TEN
PAST
NOW

Damien Lutz

CONTENTS

The Motherhood Effect

I lay back on the birthing table as robotic arms extended down from the ceiling and swung into position at my feet.

Corin, the Donor, touched the nose of her anxious face to the viewing window, twin upside-down cones misting the glass. She had visited several times during the gestation period and spoke about herself and her problems. She had touched my stomach and talked to her baby as if I were not there, growing more indifferent to me as the birth approached. I could have been invisible, my womb floating there on its own. But that was my role, what

I had been born to do, to be a vehicle for the Outsider's paternal happiness.

I watched Nurse Theene tap on the terminal next to me, as I had many times in my employ at the facility. Excelling in my training, I had provided three healthy babies for the barren Outsiders. Not like Ya Ru, who had given birth to a stillborn. I hadn't seen her again, and I doubted there was much use for a failed surrogate on the Outside. With my perfect record, and the Outsider's ever-increasing reliance on the facility, I was sure to remain in service and provide many more babies for the Donors.

The contractions began. Implementing my training, I quickly controlled their rhythm. Within an hour, I pushed the baby out onto the table.

From behind the window, Corin put a hand to her mouth, her eyes on her child, a solitary tear meandering down her cheek. She would not look at me again. That was how it had always been.

The robotic arms swooped in to clamp, cut and tie the umbilical cord. They picked up the infant and held him in front of me—his puffy body coated in waxy, cheese-like clots—in preparation for Nurse Theene to wrap him. But the terminal beeped in alarm, a red light flashed, and she remained at the machine checking data. She gestured to the arms to place the baby on my abdomen.

As I rested a hand on his wet and squirming body to stop him from rolling off, he looked up at me through half-squinted eyes, his irises the same diamond grey as my own. Our eyes connected, and a whoosh of energy surged though my body, almost knocking me back against the table. I floated inside myself, as if a hundred closed doors had been blown open inside me, flooding me with the light and air of a new and pristine awareness.

I froze, attempting to comprehend the experience, when Theene snatched up the baby and wrapped him in a towel. An unexpected desire to reach out and hold him assailed me, but Theene carried him to the window and held him up to Corin like a prize.

Still covering her mouth and crying, Corin pressed her hand against the window and stared at the boy. Theene smiled and walked off toward the bonding room. Corin moved down the hall to meet her there, leaving a hand print of heat fading from the glass.

Watching the small bundle disappear, I flooded with a longing sensation that I was never supposed to experience.

I lay there, listening intently to the child's honest cries from the next room, until the arms finished attending to me. The auto-table wheeled me out of the birthing chamber and down the hall where Grayson, the post-natal technician, waited to assess me.

The birthing room door slid shut behind, severing the child's cries from my world. But the strange experience the baby's eyes exposed me to did not leave me. It only intensified. That brief moment had somehow expanded the parameters of my world, of what I had supposed was possible, within me and without. By the time the auto-table positioned me before Grayson, a longing to hold the child pulled at me with the gravity of a sun spiralling asteroids into its core.

"Well Done, Ti La," Grayson commended, placing his phone on the desk below a wall-wide monitor and standing over my lower body. "Another healthy product. You are making us a mint."

He attached probes to my body, and my data displayed on the wall. I remained still, but a maelstrom stormed inside me. The data on the screens spiked.

"Woah, what's going on there?" he asked the graphs.

As he tapped on the keyboard on his desk, his phone chimed, and he answered it.

"Hey. No. Ti's got an anomaly. I'll keep her here overnight and double-check things in the morning. I gotta get Jimmy to fly-puck practice before six."

He put his phone in his pocket, stood up, and pulled on his jacket.

"Don't go anywhere, Ti," he said as walked out of the room. The door slid behind him, and the overhead lights dimmed, leaving me alone with the glow of my own data.

With just the humming of the monitor as company, I stood up and approached the terminal. Remembering what I had learned from watching Theene and Grayson, I navigated my way through the operating system until I found the file I was looking for. According to the file, Corin, a single parent, lived in Summer Tower in the city west. A pixelated image of the baby's face formed on the wall, and his name typed out below it.

Gus. She named him Gus.

I lay back on the table and pictured myself holding Gus against my chest, standing at an apartment window, looking at the Outside. I had never seen the Outside, but I had listened to Donors talk about their life beyond the facility, and had pieced snippets together to form an approximation of what it may look like. I imagined this scenario until the next morning—I could even see the heat from Gus' breath form a tiny patch of steam on the window—when Grayson returned and double-checked my data. The anomaly had gone, and he released me back into the schedule.

The facility was extremely pleased with my success and the speed of my recuperation. Within a month, Theene impregnated me with my fifth child, but I could not stop thinking about Gus, and his eyes. The small creature had broken into a fortress that the facility had built inside me. I checked his file any time facility staff left me alone in check-up or near a terminal. They were none the wiser, never expecting a docile Surrogate to inquire beyond its role, beyond the facility.

In the following months, the Donors visited and spoke to me as if I would always matter in their lives, but their early eagerness disappeared fairly quickly. My own usual ease of learnt response to make them feel comfortable became difficult. I could not comprehend what was happening to me, swamped by a powerfully unquestionable maternal instinct that all my training told me I was never meant to know. Something fundamental had shifted inside my thoughts. The Donors were mere providers of required materials. I was the maker. This child was mine.

Four months passed and I was starting to show. The baby moved inside me for the first time. Monitors beeped, approximating the date of birth, and the many tests began. Shortly after, I overheard Nurse Theene inform the Donors to expect a girl.

I grew unstable, tormented by the reality of the ruthlessness of my life. I knew that by the time the Donor parents pressed their indifferent faces against the viewing window to watch the birth, I would never see the girl again.

Over the next few months, various problems arose with my new baby, and Grayson grew as indifferent with me as the Donors. The estimated date of birth came and went. By the time the contractions arose, neither Grayson nor Theene were speaking to me.

The birthing table auto-wheeled me into the chamber, and Theene fluttered around me, checking my stats and flooding me with various proteins and medicines. But when the child came, it did not cry, and it did not move. The Donor's eager faces melted into despair as they turned away and hugged each other. Theene flicked off the terminal and the arms took the stillborn away. Traumatised, I reached out, but the auto-table wheeled me down the hall.

With my condition unstable, Grayson left me overnight in the check-up room. He probably didn't want to waste time with me anymore. I thought of Ya.

I waited until enough time had passed that all the staff would have left. After I waited a little longer until I could be sure the night-shift nurse would have settled and gone to sleep in her secure dorm—the way she always did—I climbed off the table to reach the terminal and brought up Gus' file. He was doing well, bonding with his Donor mother, and yet to say his first word.

I touched the image of his face flickering on the wall.

My baby.

In that moment, as the meaningless of my life almost drowned me, I saw its potential. It was a small, insignificant, almost impossible future, but I desperately wanted to realize it.

I pulled the waist-tie tight on my modesty robe, let myself out of the room and stepped silently into the corridor. I followed the thin blue tubes shedding dim light along the ceiling until I came to a large, glassine room bounded by floor-to-ceiling windows and doors. Beyond them sprouted what I could only assume was the Outside.

It was far more beautiful than I had ever imagined, like a giant monitoring machine turned inside out with all its circuitry laid bare. So much space between the doorway and the next walls, wider than fifty facility corridors.

I approached the glass entrance and the doors opened. A confusion of exotic sounds hypnotised me, luring me over the threshold and into the Outside. The doors shut behind and flashed red as they locked.

There was no going back. There was nothing to go back to.

I took one step forward and gazed about. Giant structures, dotted with squares of dark or light, towered over me in claustrophobic clusters. Walkways connected the towers, and conveyor-like vehicles slid between them along cables. Lights swept through the air attached to machines that flew.

Above and beyond the heavy confusion, and seemingly more distant than I could comprehend, pin-pricks of light twinkled in a sea of darkness.

Sky.

Terrified and exhilarated by the overwhelming strangeness, I ran, down into the ceiling-less corridors weaving between the tower bases. I kept to darker pathways, out of sight, to the west, to Summer Tower. I knew the address, and the apartment number. I'd read it every time I'd logged onto Gus' file.

I travelled several blocks when a faint whooping noise emerged from the air above me. Shadows of flying machines came up from behind and splashed red and blue light over the walls. I pressed closer into the shadows, until the lights disappeared, and I continued west.

I reached Summer Tower as the sun rose over the distant horizon, a gleaming slip peeking through the towers and floodlighting the home of my baby in gold.

A man exited sliding doors on ground level, and they remained open behind him. I strode across the courtyard—the man staring at me, but not stopping—and made it inside the tower before the doors closed.

I attempted accessing the lifts, but they would not work without some sort of authorisation. Back in the facility, when the power had gone down, we had used the stairs, so I located the tower's internal stairways, and headed up. Reaching the twenty-seventh level, I pushed through the door and looked around. A bold red thirteen stood out on the dark door at the end of the corridor.

Without a strategy, but drawn by an exquisitely undeniable force, I walked down to the door and pushed the access button. A muffled chime rang through the dawn silence on the other side. Within a minute, the shuffling of feet neared, and the door slid open a few centimeters, revealing a strip of Corin's porcelain face, and one blue eye. Her eyeball flicked up and down at me.

"Can I help you?"

"Hello. You probably don't remember me."

"No, I don't. What the hell do you want? It's six in the morning."

"I want to see Gus. I want to see my baby."

Her eyelids spread apart, eyelashes starfishing, and her eyeball seemed to swell in its socket. Pre-empting her next move, I gripped the edge of the door and held it tight. She punched the close button, and the door shot forward, wedging my fingers between it and the wall. My skin split back, revealing the metal structure of my hand. The door squealed, but I held it fast and slowly pushed it back open.

"Oh, my god," Corin exclaimed, backing away.

My arm's internal mechanics screamed as I forced the door aside enough to reach in and hit the open button. The door pulled back and I stepped through. Corin's body shook with terror, her eyes unable to leave me.

"Get the hell out of my house!"

She yelled more commands at me to stop, and my programming should have forced me to obey. But all I could think of were Gus' eyes, and holding him.

Corin darted down the hallway and out of view, most likely to get to a comm-panel she could reach. I punched the one next to the doorway to disable the system. Sparks flew out, singeing the skin on my hand and forearm. Burning skin peeled back, and a stray sunray reflected off my metal substrate. Doubt froze me. I questioned my right to hold Gus. But a faint infant cry from somewhere in the apartment called to my response system and broke the spell of my uncertainty.

I walked down the hall toward the glass-walled front room, where the morning light illuminated dust slow-dancing in the air. Corin tapped furiously onto a comm-panel.

"Hello? Emergency! Hell—"

She looked up at me and stopped, her face a world of horror. Her eyes flicked from me to something behind, and then back. I looked around. In the next room sat a white crib at the end of a bed.

"No!" she screamed, lunging at me. "Leave my baby alone!"

But I was faster. I darted into the bedroom, shut the door and locked it. Corin pounded on the door, screaming incoherently. A faint cry floated out of the crib. I approached its side. Gus stared up at me through his beautiful, crystal-grey eyes.

The pounding on the door stopped and other voices arose.

"What's going on, ma'am?"

"The surrogate droid," Corin screamed. "She's got my baby!"

The pounding resumed, and the other voices called out new commands to me.

"Give me back my baby!" Corin cried out. "He's mine! He's my baby!"

But she may as well have been in another dimension. I lifted Gus from the crib and cradled him against my bosom. I made noises that came from some random algorithm; I cooed and purred, like a wild mammal in a cave with her young. Gus settled and reached up to my face. He stroked my lips with his tiny fat fingers and uttered two syllables.

"Muh-muh."

I carried him to the window and stared at the beautiful Outside. Heat from Gus's breath steamed the glass. I held him close, until a familiar whooping noise emerged outside, and red and blue lights flashed in his eyes.

Ocean's Agent

Author's Note: I've always been fascinated with short stories, or infographics, that sum up a vast history. Written in the early 1990s, this was my creative interpretation of the evolution of humankind, with a suggestion for the meaning of our existence.

———

Sometime after the volcanic tectonics settled into a sphere of slow-shifting land mass, an anemone formed in the ocean and waited for the continental crust to cool.

As tidal rhythms rocked the pulsating bell of the sea, something called down to the anemone, something separate from the planetary rock to which its ocean home clung.

Peering through the fish-eye view of its surface, the transparent sea creature followed a disc of light parading through the black head of heaven. The lunar being above waxed and waned, teasing like a galactic Jezebel, undressing and redressing. The anemone gazed, amazed.

What are you?

Mesmerized by mystery, the agent of the ocean washed itself ashore to view, dry-eyed, the full moon lighting the dark, but star-studded, sky. In that moment, between ocean and star, the anemone committed to reaching the blinding jewel and unearthing all its secrets.

To protect itself from sunlight spears, and an array of relentless elements assailing it on land, the anemone developed a shell around its neon-gel self. To move and maneuver, it sprouted limbs of skeleton and nerve-laced muscle, and set up senses across its surface.

But these mere self-expansions were not enough. If it were to catch the moon in its net of knowing, the anemone would need to multiply and mutate, and so it evolved mouth, teeth, tongue, and genitalia.

The dinosaur was not the anemone's first attempt to reach the moon, but typical of the infantile stage its thought had reached. Growing to enormous size, it believed it could stretch out its long neck and eat the moon. But the dinosaur grew too large for its environment and ate itself into oblivion.

The anemone retreated to an earlier lizard form, but could not get up off its lazy, cold-blooded belly. Birds were a brilliant metamorphosis, but it did not anticipate the lack of oxygen in the ozone, forgetting its dreams as it flew mindlessly through the stratosphere.

Bored by failure and the drain of time, the anemone resided in its mammal forms, ebbing into a docile, earth-loving nature, too grounded for any space travel. Until one specie—the ape—began digging at the ground with it's hairy fingers, unearthing and consuming food and water high in metallic elements. They brimmed with excess energy, and their highly magnetized bodies sensed the pull of the moon ever more intensely.

Its lunar dream reawakened, the anemone knew it had found its vehicle in the ore-addicted human.

Like radar towers unfolding themselves, the radiated sapiens stood upright in anticipation, and their body hair fell. They invented useful items and learnt how to cultivate and store food to sustain and perpetuate their evolution. The naked apes sketched their enhanced visions in sand and stone, inventing languages to share the holograms in their minds, articulating the micro and macro aspects of planetary dances.

In a crystallizing infestation, the human organism took apart the Earth's natural structures, mixed and matched the elements in its quest to understand it all, and took control of the world.

As its numbers grew, the anemone constructed politics and religion, putting the docile populace to work. Digging bigger holes in search of more metal, it shaped the tools, built the engines, and constructed the wings. In a climatic rush of technological advancement, the anemone, in its skin and bone suit, manifested the ship that reached the moon and stuck its starry label upon the rock's bare and meteor-battered surface. Conquering the off-world enigma, the human ego rejoiced through televisions all over the world.

But after the initial rush of the first footprint, a certain uncertainty laid naked upon the shore of it all. Having reached its dream, the anemone found nothing but a dead and empty asteroid.

Where are my answers? Why am I here?

In a glorious moment of revelation, the moon and Earth tilted in their timeless waltz. The sun dipped behind the earth, it's final rays splashing off the ocean, across space, and through the anemone's solar visor, enlightening the wayward sea-creature's mind.

I am a seed.

The anemone, following its oceanic blueprint, had evolved the species as nothing but separate stages of the ocean's ever-spiraling evolution, to be dropped away when done like those of a rocket, to free the ocean from its planetary prison.

But what now?

From the lunar surface many miles from its ocean home, nestled in the skull of its human contraption, and reliant on technological extensions, the anemone gazed back at the Earth.

Cities twinkled radioactive webs in their sprawl across the continents. Satellites twirled like dervishes in solo orbits around the globe. On the lunar surface, the ship's lights flashed on and off as if chatting with each other. The radar dish spun like a little moon DJ mixing cosmic beats.

The sun disappeared behind the earth in the first solar eclipse seen from the moon, and the anemone understood.

To continue the ocean's quest, it was time to evolve out of its archaic human contraption, slip into something more adaptable—more mechanical—and abort the fragile fish-bowl atmosphere it had consumed.

For only by inhabiting the cyborg machines of the ocean's latest designs, would the anemone be free to abort the planet in pursuit of its lonely mystery:

Are there other oceans out there?

Sink Hole

Author's Note: We can't be sure if the increase of reported sink holes early this century was because there are more, or because there were more people with cameras and internet. Regardless, the thought of an armada of these unpredictable phenomena suddenly opening up and heading towards a city...well, it was too Hollywood-Armageddon-blockbuster to take seriously. But it was also too fun not to write about it, and that's how this quirky tale was born.

I had all I needed—my own tent in a dry spot under the bridge, out of the wind and rain, and two mattresses to stop most of the cold coming up out of the ground. I had all I needed to wait for The End.

Afternoon shadows reached into the park with their dark, chilly fingers. A breeze flapped our huddle of tents. Traffic roared across the overpass, and a train rattled through the ravine below, shaking the ground.

I sat by the walkway and watched the pedestrian surge of Cogs on their way home from their jobs in the Machine. I recognized their faces, every one of them. Different versions of my own, before hopelessness had overwhelmed me.

I'd traveled the world, blogging about the impact eight billion lives had upon the planet. It didn't take a rocket scientist to work out that equaled one big earth-eating machine. But no matter how many photos of damaged lands I shared, or how many vanishing species I reported, the Cogs were too busy being busy to care. Eventually, futility stole over my soul. I hid away in this invisible pocket to wait for the inevitable End.

"You there!" chirped a voice next to me. "Happy Tuesday! Wanna go steal somethin'?"

It was Vlad. He was the only one in the park who had introduced himself, but I kept my distance. You can never get too close to a kleptomaniac without eventually losing everything you own. He'd 'explore' the few belongings right out of my tent if I wasn't vigilant.

I shook my head. "No, thanks. I'm waiting for The End."

He scrunched his face, and his white beard ruffled like a cloud snagged on a rock. "And what if the end don't get here 'till tomorrow? Or the next day?" He huffed and disappeared down the street.

I returned to the huddle of tents to find Tooey sitting by the fire bin, tweaking the dial on his radio like it was some hooker's nipple. I sat by the warmth, rolled a number, and listened to the Zen white-noise of the static.

Over the next freezing hour, the park's inhabitants emerged from their tents and settled around the fire with Tooey and I. Even Jasmine joined us; she normally stayed by her tent, hosting one of her imaginary tea parties. (Vlad said Jasmine used to be a socialite, but she rarely socialized with us.) Seeing her face by the flames warmed the colder parts in me that the fire's heat couldn't reach.

Flames crackled as their edges extinguished into smoke and slid up toward the stars. Tooey found music on his radio, and a moth fluttered around the bent aerial. Jim Morrison sang about climbing through the tide on a Moonlight Drive, when a high-voiced newsreader interrupted with a story about the ever-increasing sink holes. Before he finished, however, his voice cut out, and Tooey barked at the radio.

"Serves ya right! All that diggin' and drillin' and frackin'. That's what yer get playin' Jenga with the planet."

I smoked another number so I could forget about the sink holes and the cogs and the planet, and just sleep. That was the extent of my activities, and that was just fine. When you don't believe in the future, you have a lot less to care about.

I remember standing and stumbling toward my tent, until the rest disappeared in a descending haze.

*****

The first thought alighting on my waking mind was how lovely and quiet the world had become. No traffic roared across the bridge above. No train rumbled past in the ravine below. But as soon as that thought appeared, a thumping pain stampeded into my head and chased the quiet away.

I shuffled my position and grass scratched my face, alerting me to the absence of my mattress. I pried my eyes open—the morning sun so bright and glaring I wanted to slap it—and found myself laying down by the train tracks. In my stupor the previous night, I had stumbled too close to the ravine's edge, toppled down the side, and passed out in the bushes.

Climbing out of the ravine, I shuffled back to the tents to find no one around, except Jasmine. She chattered away on her blanket, hosting another imaginary function. I raised my hand to wave when I saw Vlad hauling the mattress from my tent.

"Hey!" I yelled. "Get outta there!"

Vlad jumped as if he'd seen a ghost. "I thought you'd gone," he shot back. "With all the others."

"What do you mean? Where is everyone?"

"Last night, the evacuation."

"Evacuation? What are you talking about?"

Vlad narrowed his eyes. "The sink holes are comin'. Trucks came in the night to round us up. They took everyone away. But not me. I hid." He smiled a cheeky smile, betraying his excitement at having an entire city to pillage.

I asked about Jasmine.

"They tried to drag her away, too, but she wasn't leaving in the middle of her party. She put up a pretty good fight."

Jasmine waved and smiled.

So there it was. The End. It was finally coming.

"Let's go steal something'," suggested Vlad, a wide grin splitting open his white beard.

"No, thank you. I'll just sit here and wait for The End. Can't be long now."

Vlad huffed and disappeared into the city to rob the world. I sat down to enjoy the quiet bounty of my surrender.

Hours passed, and I grew impatient. As the sun reached its zenith, I was sure the silence would drown me, when a horn blared. A silver motor home, with its sunroof popped, sped down the empty street like a bullet on wheels. The vehicle bounced over the footpath and skidded to halt in front of me, and Vlad stuck his bald head out of the driver's window.

"Well, don't just sit there, let's go see it!"

I stared back in bewildered silence.

"The End!" he exclaimed. "Let's go see these damn sink holes."

Yes, I thought, frightened and excited. All this sitting and waiting. I'll go meet The End and get this over and done with.

I called to Jasmine to join us, but she gasped and clutched imaginary pearls.

"What would my guests think of me if I left in the middle of my party?"

I envied her self-delusion as I stepped into the van.

Vlad drove the first few kilometers, pushing the engine as hard as he could, until the road gave way to fields of grass and rock, forcing him to slow down. Bored by the universe's speed limit, he asked me to take over the wheel. I obliged, allowing him to play with the dashboard. He pushed buttons like a blind man trying to play a juke box, until he accidentally activated the vehicle's artificial intelligence.

"Hello, I'm Ava, your Automobile Virtual Assistant. Where would you like to go today?"

Vlad whooped and slapped the dashboard, as if he'd just found the Hope Diamond. I asked him to shut it off, but he was too excited at discovering another companion on board.

"Hello! I'm Vlad. And this—" Vlad looked at me and stopped. I'd never told him my name, but I didn't see any point in sharing it then, not that close to The End, and certainly not with a thief and a machine.

I screwed up my face, gripped the wheel and scanned the horizon for sink holes. As Vlad flirted with Ava, I became more determined than ever to drive us straight into the abyss.

We knew when the sinkholes were near, not by what we could see, but by what we couldn't. The mountainous landscape disappeared in chunks before our eyes, like an invisible, monstrous child munched on a row of giant Oreos. Then we heard them— hollow, gurgling gulps swallowing up the world.

I chickened out at the first sinkhole. I veered off on approach and drove around its crumbling edge, gaping at the still black ocean of nothing. Vlad whistled and rested his head against the window.

"Well, ain't that just the most beautiful thing you ever did see?"

But it wasn't. It was terrifying. My own fathomless fear and despair stared back at me. I wanted to drive off the futile rollercoaster of life, but I couldn't let go. I cursed my cowardice, when a rumble reverberated through the ground and shook the van. My stomach caved in on itself and I clutched the wheel, as the van sailed off the collapsing ground and into a giant sinkhole yawning open beneath us.

Vlad threw his arms in the air and screamed with joy. I stopped breathing, yet a certain satisfaction danced in the core of my terror, a rejoicing that the waiting was over, and the inevitable End had, finally, come.

The End, however, took longer to transpire than I expected.

Vlad stopped yelping, running out of breath. I stopped holding mine, my lungs forcing me to draw in air. Going by the clock on the vehicle's dashboard, we'd been falling for almost fifteen minutes.

"Ava!" I yelled above the roar of the wind. "Are we going to crash or not?"

"Taking our coordinates into consideration," she explained in her polite, synthesized voice, "and the perpendicular angle of our descent, we should collide with the center of the earth in approximately one minute and twelve seconds."

She counted down. The air grew hotter and harder to breathe. Our plummet accelerated, and the van's sides buckled and contorted. I braced myself for the collision with the center of the Earth, but we flew straight through it.

For a split second, everything felt upside down. An invisible force spun the van, floating us in a zero-gravity moment, and then shot us up toward the other side of the world.

"It appears we are in a Gravity Tunnel," explained Ava, "formed by a sink hole extending from one side of the planet to the other."

"A gravity funnel!" Vlad cheered.

"You don't even know what that is!" I retorted like a child, disappointment riddling me. How long would this ride go on for?

"According to my calculations," continued Ava, "in fourteen minutes and three seconds, we will emerge from the sink hole in Southern Spain."

"Spain!" cheered Vlad, slapping me on the back. "I've always wanted to meet a Señorita!"

Light twinkled in the dark around us, emerging as waterfalls in the distance. Droplets appeared and bombarded the windscreen. Mist and light filled the air. We were nearing the surface.

With a sudden whoosh, the van burst out of the sink hole and shot up into the sky above the other side of the world.

Spanning the panoramic view of the driver's cabin, a spectacularly decimated landscape stretched below us, filled in by burst oceans and crumbling mountains. It was a beautiful tragedy, as if the planet had had enough of humanity nibbling at its edges and simply started eating back.

Gravity slowed the mobile home to a gentle stop mid-air, and then pulled it back down. My stomach lurched, and I screamed again. We plummeted, and all my frustrations fears engulfed me with a terrifying enormity. I missed my tent. I wanted to see

Jasmine again. I screamed and I screamed, until the force of the fall yanked the terror out of me and flung it behind to flutter off into the dark. I looked at Vlad, and we burst into laughter.

As we plunged back down the sink hole, waters from the remnants of the Mediterranean ocean burst over the edge and chased after us. My heart pounded. For the first time in years, I didn't want The End to come.

Passing through the center of the world for the second time, the van spun again and buckled in further, like a soda can crushed in an invisible giant's fist.

"Ava," I yelled. "How do we get out of this?"

"If my calculations are correct—" A dent collapsed in the dashboard, and Ava's voice frazzled and cut out like the newsreader on Tooey's radio. Vlad fell silent. My heart slowed. The pitta patta of the chasing ocean drummed a meditative rhythm on the bottom of the van. In my clarity, I realized there was really only one thing to do.

"Come on, Vlad." I slapped him on the back and led him to the sunroof. The wind pushed back on us as we climbed out onto the top of the van. The bright surface of the sink hole above grew larger. Or was it below? I wasn't sure anymore. All I knew was that I was alive, and I had a few seconds left to make the most of it.

We clutched the roof racks as the van burst out of the sink hole. I turned to Vlad and yelled through the wind, "I'm Stan."

Vlad smiled. "Good to meet ya, Sam."

I laughed and took a deep breath. "Are you ready?" He nodded.

As the gravity slowed the van's ascent to pivot point, we stood up, stepped to the edge, and jumped.

*****

I woke with a jolt. I shuffled my position, and grass scratched my face, alerting me to the absence of my mattress. I pried my eyes open—the morning sun so bright and glaring I wanted to slap it—and found myself laying down by the train tracks. In my stupor the previous night, I had stumbled too close to the ravine's edge, toppled down the side, and passed out in the bushes.

Traffic roared across the overpass, and my head thumped from too much smoke the night before. The faint memory of a dream teased my mind, but I couldn't grasp it. A train rattled the tracks, and my heart beat a little drum. I jumped to my feet, scrambled up the ravine, and shuffled back to the tents.

The sounds and smells of the world teased my senses into a delightful confusion. Jasmine sat on her rug, laughing with her imaginary friends. Tooey tweaked his radio by the smoking fire bin as he searched for another elusive station. The Cogs marched past in their morning migration with a beautiful rhythm I had never noticed before.

"You there!" chirped a voice from behind. Vlad's impossibly-happy, bearded grin appeared by my side. "Happy Wednesday. Wanna go steal somethin'?"

As I opened my mouth to decline, I felt the faint tendrils of the dream let go of my mind. An uplifting coolness flared in my chest, blooming into something so foreign and diamond-rare to me that it took me a moment to recognize it as hope.

It was a beautiful, noisy, busy day—far too perfect to waste sitting around waiting for The End.

Sea of Ingenuity

Sea of Ingenuity was written in the early 1990's, and was first published in the Anything Goes Anthology, Volume 2 in 2015.

When the hijacked moon orbiting our Ark slipped into its first lunar eclipse, babies just being born failed to breathe. Scientists stuck their cold, steel stethoscopic probes into our pregnant women, only to find fetuses floating lifeless in embryonic fluid, their tiny human hearts never to beat.

Astronomer-engineers informed us that while the moon we'd stolen from the Earth was awash with the copper shadow of the Ark, unexpected forces had acted upon it, turning it 180 degrees and facing it's dark side toward us. Perhaps, in our rush to build the Ark to escape the failing Earth, we'd missed something vital.

The gigantic, spherical structure of the Ark, and the ecosystems we replicated inside it, were hailed as a living, breathing testament to our genius. We simulated magnetic poles and harmonized them perfectly with the artificial climate generated by the wind and wave machines. The animals, insects and plants we introduced maintained the flow of the life-force throughout the Ark. And in a moment of crowning glory, to maintain the rhythms of life, we stole the moon from the dying Earth's gravity, and re-started its monthly orbit around the Ark. As the first New Lunar Eclipse approached, we celebrated, toasting our intelligence, too blinded by our brilliance to understand we'd broken the connection between earth and life.

Even after the moon moved out from under the Ark's shadow, our existence continued to lose meaning. Parents cried dry tears as their young girls—their pale, delicate, little sweethearts— stopped bleeding, but failed to fall pregnant. Despairing mothers took to wandering our constructed world in a silent daze, their eyes dull and dry, limbs limp and lagging. It was as if the moon mourned the dying Earth we'd left behind, and opened up a vast, barren emptiness inside them. Their children gathered at the artificial ocean and waited by the wave machine, pining for their mothers to return.

The scientists promised that our frozen fertility resources would reproduce under controlled conditions. They did not. In response, our spiritual guardians wielded words of gloom and guilt. "We warned this destiny would descend upon us for tampering with the Divine!"

Without fertility accessible to us, without the ability to perpetuate life, the Gravity Machine barely held us back from floating away in our emptiness. In the depths of our depression, our senses diminished. Sounds became dull and flat, and music was abandoned. Smells seemed to vanish. Taste became a forgotten sensation and we lost interest in eating. Opportunistic ills took hold. Many fell sick, their bodies refusing to heal, and the Ark's maintenance systems broke down from lack of care.

I sit here now, on the maintenance platform of a still turbine, to be above the heavy solemnity. I gaze through the sky-shield to the distant moon, its Sea of Ingenuity blank before me, and I wonder where we went wrong. Should we not have given up on the Earth? But we could not fix what we had broken. The Ark was our promise to our children to restore the hope for the future that had deserted them. Hope for the future has always driven us. While there is hope, there remains a spark of the life-force.

I rub my stomach. How long I will live I cannot say, but I will not have my unborn surgically removed. I will not have them probed and tested. Enough of all our dissecting implements and genius interferences. I call her Mia. I call him Michael. I call myself Mother.

This I leave, should you, our dream, find this recording. I leave you these words as a sign of the persistent urge that drives me to speak, holding back my hand from halting my own life. For some reason—perhaps beyond it—as I look up at the once far-side of the Moon now alight in bright starlight, I find, even amongst all this misery, I am, like a child, still staring up and hoping.

The Furnace

Author's Note: A recurring theme in my work is artificial intelligence becoming self-aware. Not an original theme, of course, but as it is yet to happen—and we seem to be sure it will—there is so much to speculate on. My interests lie in how an AI might experience more metaphysical phenomena, such as love, companionship, dreams, and near-death experiences.

Outnumbered by the stars above, tiny lights twinkled in the dark terrain far below me. I plummeted through twilight toward the valley, the wind whistling through the gaps in my body.

"OK, buddy, prepare to go dark." Using the nickname he'd given me, my remote-pilot's voice betrayed his emotion. Human sentimentality was the main reason their soldiers had been replaced by my kind. "You two are on your own from here."

"Copy. Rendezvous at zero-four-zero-zero-hours." Maneuvering myself into a neutral free fall position, I shut down communications and lowered the light of my internal display. Spot, my four-legged robot counterpart, curled up in its own free fall, ten meters to my left, and dropped fast. I activated Spot's parachute, then my own. With a whoosh, the chute deployed, yanking me out of my plunge and settling into a gentle fall.

As the edges of my parachute fluttered like a flock of crows, the ground raced up to meet me. My feet struck the rocky ground with a crunch. I threw myself sideways to distribute the landing shock, and rolled back onto my feet. Before my chute could touch the ground, I hit the recoil button and whisked it into my back compartment. Spot trotted up and stood at the ready beside me.

My algorithms assessed the data flowing in from the surroundings, modeling a 3D environment, and optimizing my strategy. Although the sun had set hours ago, my sensors noted heat still rising from the ground, like the warmth released from a recently killed body. Reconfigured to local conditions, I set out for my target, Spot trailing behind.

After running for several minutes across the valley base, Spot and I ascended the rocky foothill. Almost at the zenith, a snap and a crunch came from behind. Red lights flickered across my internal display. I spun around to find Spot on its side, three legs running in the air. Racing to the confused droid's side, I assessed the damage. Spot's left hind leg had been caught in a rusty foot trap. (A devious and unexpected booby trap, I knew I had to be extra cautious from there on). The leg's hydraulics had been pierced, and blue oil spat out onto the dry ground. With the damage irreparable, I switched off the struggling droid's engine. I took the spare ammunition cartridges it was carrying for me and loaded them into my compartments, until I calculated any more added weight might slow down my responses. I set Spot's self-destruct for thirty minutes to prevent the technology falling into the enemy's hands, yet enough time for me to complete my mission.

Continuing up the hill, I reached the top and crouched. Two hundred meters ahead, the silhouette of the dilapidated compound stood like a huddle of homeless giants under the stars. I activated stealth mode, sneaked up to the compound's wall, and threw up a grapple to latch on to the top edge. Scaling the crumbling surface with ease, I peered over and scanned the area.

Through the navy and fluorescent green of my night vision, I identified four guards patrolling the yard, each one dressed in long shirts and baggy pants, and carrying a rifle. A figure exited the out-house and shuffled toward the main building: a boy, limping, most likely a victim of the many air strikes my Commanders had conducted. Intel had not advised children were in the strike zone. But the enemy was not defined by age.

I knew my target's location: third floor, second door on the right. At the precise moment the guards were farthest away, I dashed across the yard toward the rear of the main building, and stopped at a barred window. Using the laser tool embedded in my forearm, I silently severed the bars, sliced a whole in the glass, and climbed through.

After a brief pause to scan the shadowy interior, I generated a 3D model in my navigation system, and used it to guide me through the darkened house. Following it up a staircase toward my target's quarters, I reached the point of no return. Intel had warned that heavy steel doors blocked the top of the stairwell on the first and second-floor landings. From there on in, things got noisy.

Reaching the first steel doors, I set explosives, stood back, and blew them off their hinges. Walking through the billowing dust, I noted figures scattering into rooms, clearing my path to the next staircase. I ascended the stairs, and blew the second doors. Someone wailed hysterically. Burqa-clad figures ran out of their rooms, screaming into the hallway. I pushed past their waving arms, stepped over a woman with a piece of debris protruding from her leg, and entered my target's room.

A single candle burned, standing on a small plate, in the middle of the room. Several figures scattered to the walls, betrayed by their shadows.

Discarded clothes and blankets littered the floor. I spied my target lying on a mattress in the corner of the room. He was old and thin. I raised my weapon, and heard the bullet slide into position.

It was to be a simple, straightforward, professional hit. But just before I pulled the trigger, I realized my mistake. Sensing movement above, I stepped back to face the person hiding in the ceiling beams, but the extra ammunition I carried slowed down my reaction time. Feet collided with my head, the impact knocking me off balance and to the floor. My assailant hit the floorboards beside me, accompanied by a peculiar heavy thud. Before I could react, something long and metallic drove deep into my left optic. That is when my entire system shut down for 1.2 seconds, and the following sequence recorded in my memory:

Surrounded by total darkness, the solid ground opened up beneath me, swallowing me whole, and collapsing back over on top of me. Unable to move under the weight of the burial, I could nonetheless feel myself being sifted down through the soil. Every tiny grain shifted with delicate precision, ushering me deeper underground. The sifting hastened, like the last grains of sand rushing through the neck of an hourglass, until, all at once, I fell freely, as a drop in a curtain of rain. I plummeted for so long I ceased to sense gravity, losing all sense of direction in the weightlessness. Just when I sensed something approaching, I smashed into solidity with an elephantine thud.

The violent collision recoiled a sense of bearing back into my system, like a star collapsing in on itself. I lay stunned and stared up into the high shadows.

A spark flashed, twinkled, and fell towards me. Mesmerized, I watched the object fall all the way down, twisting and growing larger and closer, until the surety of it hitting me snapped me out of my paralysis. I rolled out of the way, as the object landed with an echoing ping beside my head. I turned to find a bullet lying silent and breathless, as if it had travelled long and far to get there. A jumbled clink sounded next to my hand—a grapple hook. I raised up on one elbow to find myself on a bare patch of flat, black rock in the middle of a vast, dark chamber. A faint orange glow emanated from the left, silhouetting a field of high mounds. The occasional thunder of something large crashed in the distance.

Standing, I noticed the metallic pitta-patta of countless objects landing around me. Objects of various shapes and sizes, of metals and plastics, rained down from the shadows above, piling onto the dunes covering the cavern floor. Computer components, wires, broken glass screens, artificial limbs, plastic tubes, and random substrate parts all mounted under the continual rain of refuse.

Heat from the glowing area of the chamber seeped into my system, as molecules within the metal of my skeleton quivered in fear of melting. My probability algorithms made a suggestion: I had been transported to the place where all manufactured items lost, forgotten, thrown away or buried were delivered to be reborn. Ground further under the foot of the present, all objects of human invention were sifted down by Earth's gentle sand-

fingers, working the impurities into this digestive cavern deep below the surface.

My algorithms completed their scenario, surmising that not too far from where I stood, flamed the furnace of the Earth, where all things untrue and unnatural were cleansed in the heat of their burning substrates, disassembled and scattered amongst their natural elements: the gateway to invention's after-life.

Drawn toward the light, I stepped through the refuse of robot limbs and technological intestines, lulled by the sound of the fire-some waves washing over the feet of the dunes. Stumbling around the whale-size carcass of a warship, the source of heat and light revealed itself—a sprawling, lava lake.

Liquid molecules, in the metal of my skin, separated from their solid counterparts, and beaded like sweat across my burning brow. I approached the flaming lake, steam thickening the air. Silhouettes of sinking arms and legs disappeared downstream as they were ushered toward a humming, hellish glow. I could feel the heat's fury in the dark ores that had been mined to make my eyes.

Steam and the light merged, preventing me from seeing more than a meter ahead, when something bumped against my shin. A mechanical leg protruded from passing lava. I picked it up to see Spot's robotic hind leg in my hand. The wave of fire washed over my own feet, alarms ringing out across my substrate.

'What am I doing here?' I wondered.

The light intensified, suffusing my vision and engulfing me in a blinding haze, as I felt my body swept up and out of the cavern.

Screaming pierced my audio receivers.

As my system rebooted, my right optic reconfigured, and the room in the compound materialized around me. I became aware of the clang-clang-clang of objects hitting me. Seven burqa-clad women stood above me, pummeling my substrate with makeshift weapons. I could see the unidentifiable object still protruding from my left optic. Standing, I towered over my assailants. They backed away and fled the room.

A quick analysis showed my substrate remained intact—apart from my damaged optic. But I was hot, over-heated. I grasped the object protruding from my optic, and yanked it out of the socket. In my hand I held the lower half of a human's prosthetic leg, a wire from my socket fused to the leg's connector joint.

Just as I resolved that the attack on my optic had caused a glitch in my Reality Schematics, steam curled up in my vision.

Smoke.

The candle had been knocked over in the scuffle, the scattered clothes catching alight. Flames licked my feet and spread across the littered floor.

I froze, my sense of reality shifting between the smoke filled room and the steaming lava cavern. In one moment, the leg in my hand belonged to the boy, in the next, it was Spot's leg.

Scanning the smoky room, I located my target, an old man crouching on the bed in the corner, hiding behind a one-legged boy. Standing on his shaking leg, the boy—my assailant, and who's prosthetic I held in my hand—glared at me like a wild thing, his chest heaving. The fire between us gleamed in his sharp eyes. My position prevented the boy or my target from escaping, but it was clear the boy would rather fight than flee.

Identify enemy. Eliminate target.

I raised my gun. My targeting system hovered over the old man's face, jumped to the boy, and then back to the old man. It refused to lock on. I checked my directives, but they had not changed.

The boy's heart rate and body language betrayed his desperate fear of losing the old man he protected.

With my targeting system functioning normally, and no fault in my directives, I found the problem: my definition of 'enemy'. The concept of having been so close to my own death infiltrated my algorithms, confused their rationale, and evoked a compassionate response in me that I usually reserved for allies.

The boy's leg quivered, losing its strength, and he fell against the wall. My targeting focused on the old man's grubby face, yet I still could not pull the trigger.

Conflicted by the deeper understanding of the consequences of my kill, I struggled to fulfill my directive. In my collision of realties, the exposure to such a personal sense of mortality had caused a fundamental reconfiguration of my awareness. 'Enemy' had lost meaning. The mortal destiny all life shared in this world made us all allies.

Enemy not determined.

With my killer directive compromised, I lowered my gun and approached the defiant boy. He arched up, like a cat, terror in his eyes, lips pulled back in a snarl. I placed his prosthetic leg at his good foot. As I backed away, the flames eating the room flickered in his pupils, and his face disappeared into light and smoke.

Aborting my mission, I escaped the confusion of the compound and headed back the way I had come. I calculated I had twelve minutes to reach Spot, deactivate his self-destruct, and take him home.

Berg

Tim, Matty and I were fishing on the jetty when the iceberg floated into the bay. There wasn't much left of it, but it was still a Goliath of ice. The translucent traveller just drifted in as if looking for a place to berth, rivulets running down its side like sweat off a sailor's back.

As it floated nearer, the shredding of its weather-ravaged sides came into view, and the berg looked more like a drowning man being washed ashore.

Matty jumped into his tinny, yanked the cord on its 15hp motor, and sped out to our frozen visitor. He pulled his anchor out from under the seat and stabbed it into the berg's side. I winced at that. After wedging it in until just the end was exposed, he knotted a rope to the anchor and ferried the rope to us back on the jetty.

Tim and I pulled, and Matty parked the tinny to come back and help us. Together, we hauled that berg in until its slick side bumped against the planks at our feet. I felt like we'd rescued somebody.

We climbed on board like young explorers, slipping and sliding, laughing like kids. I nearly went over the side twice into the icy water. Tim made it to the top first and cheered like a hero in a movie. We laughed harder, until a frightening growl slashed the air around us, it's echo killing all other sound across the bay. We froze.

Another softer growl, but more menacing in the abrupt silence.

I wasn't sure if the image of a polar bear came into my mind before the actual beast appeared on the berg's edge, so for a few seconds I thought I was dreaming. Then it growled again, and the warmth running down my leg assured me I was awake.

The gaunt beast stood between us and the jetty, with a jaw drooling from hunger and starving, red-blood eyes.

Innocence

Author's note: The following story contains some uncomfortable subject matter, as it explores the darker side of how we perceive innocence and guilt.

Oscar Luiz clutched his father's hand as they strode out of the cold afternoon, through the sliding doors, and into the warmth of the dark foyer. As the world moved about him, he searched inside his mind for reasons why he stole the multi-vice. One thing was for certain, with all the CCTVs in the city, the police would track him down.

Can't do much to an eight-year old, he thought.

"I'm sorry, Dad."

His father responded by saying nothing, gripping his son's hand tighter, and hastening his pace, pulling Oscar across the foyer into the bright open mouth of the lift. Closing the door with a *ting*, the lift swallowed them whole.

"The Police are gonna be here soon, son. You know that, right? Face-recog everywhere."

Oscar nodded.

"They're gonna ask me why you stole it, and then what do you think they gonna say?"

Oscar didn't want to answer, the repercussions of his actions lighting up in his mind like the cigarettes of inmates in a crowded cell—an angst that never bothered him or raised an alarm in his mind until it was too late.

Oh, yeah. They can do plenty, they can take me away.

His father squeezed Oscar's hand until the flesh squashed painfully against the bones in his fingers.

"My points," Oscar blurted, wincing. "They gonna take my points."

Something on the outside of the lift clipped the shaft as it passed each level. *Tak, tak, tak.*

"And what happens when all my points are gone, son?"

Fear demanded Oscar's attention, fear of being separated from his Dad. His legs shook and his bottom lip trembled. Silent sobs heaved his chest as he held back tears.

"I'm sorry, Daddy," he blubbered. "I'm sorry, I—" But the sobs overwhelmed his words and tears broke through his stoic front. His father squeezed his hand again, but this time it was gentle and reassuring.

"You keep acting up, son, and they're gonna take you away from me. They're lookin' for any excuse. I promised your mother I wouldn't let that happen. Neither of us want that, right?'

Tak, tak, tak.

Oscar settled himself. He fisted his small hand and rubbed an eye dry. "No, Daddy. I just…I just didn't think."

"Well, you need to start thinking, son. Even an eight-year old's gotta think." *Tak, tak, tak.* "I miss your mother, too."

But Oscar didn't miss his mother. To miss her would mean he hoped she might come back. But he knew she wouldn't.

Dead people don't come back.

The lift settled at their level and the bell chimed. As the doors opened, his father scooped Oscar up in strong arms, and carried him through the inverted cones of spotlights spearing intervals into the dark corridor. Oscar hung on tight, both arms wrapped around his father's thick neck, the salty odour of sweat repulsing and yet comforting.

A squeaking emerged out of the hall silence, and an old man shuffled past them toward the lift. Oscar recognised Mr Cavanagh—the reclusive old man from number twelve at the end of the hallway—by the noisy wheel of the tartan shopping trolley he wheeled behind him. The heavy solitude exuding from the old man's stooped frame rendered him as disregardable and nondescript as the paint peeling from the walls, or the stains worn into the carpet.

Mr Luiz reached their apartment door and plonked Oscar onto his feet. Oscar kept his eyes on Mr Cavanagh. The old man stepped into the lift's bright trapezoid of cold, white light, and the door slid shut with its familiar *ting*, leaving the end of the hallway dark and empty.

"Does he have any friends?" Oscar wondered aloud.

"Who?"

"Mr Cavanagh."

His father looked up the hallway as if he hadn't noticed anyone pass them. He turned back to tap the entry code into the door panel.

"Don't know much about him, and that's the way he seems to like it. That's the way I like it. Now get inside."

He steered Oscar through the door into the tight square apartment, and pointed to the worn, two-seater couch. It sat under the window, bathed in a haze of milky light, like a giant dog sleeping in the sun. Through the dirty glass, a wall of similar windows stared back from the opposite towers, washed out by the sunlight.

Oscar slumped back into the deep couch, his short legs sticking out perpendicular to his body. He dropped his head and looked up in an attempt to look innocent—the whites of his eyes forming crescents under his dark pupils—but it only made him look as guilty as hell.

His father paced in front of him and pushed his fingers through his thinning, dark hair.

"I'm gonna do a little creative talking, son. You know what I mean by that?"

Oscar nodded.

"We gotta stick together, alright?"

Oscar nodded again. The doorbell chimed. His heart tripped.

"Visitors Constable Brant and Sargent Tate," announced the synthesized voice of the home-system. "From the Protective Services Unit. Access must be granted."

His father eyed the door, put his hands on his hips, and took in a deep breath. He flicked a hand at Oscar.

"Go to your room, and stay there."

Oscar jumped to the floor and scuttled into his room. As the door to his room auto-shut behind him, he heard the front door reopen, and the gravelly voice of one of the officers.

"Mr Luiz?"

"Yes."

"I'm Sargent Tate. This is Constable Brant. Is this you and your son?"

Their voices paused, and Oscar imagined the Sargent holding up a mobile with Oscar's face on the screen

"Yes," his father replied.

"That your son taking the multi-vice?"

"It's my fault, officer. I told him to grab one and I forgot to pay for it."

Oscar hated listening to his father lie. He didn't think his father was very convincing. To escape hearing the weak and child-like tone, Oscar climbed out of the small window and sat on the ledge—he wasn't supposed to do that either, but he liked it out there. Below him the tower dropped twenty-two floors to a wide courtyard connecting the tower bases. The disorientation of the world rising up and dropping away overwhelmed the numb emptiness that had opened up inside him since his mother had died. It made him feel normal. Stealing things, and lying… they made him feel normal. Because the rush made him feel *something*.

A light went on in the window grid on the opposite tower. Another went off. The slow, random light-show calmed him. He inhaled a deep breath of the metallic air, and exhaled. It was going to be okay.

A flash of red to his left caught his attention; a curtain flapped out of an open window at the end of the tower. A ledge, sticking out almost half an arm's length, ran between the apartment windows. He suddenly remembered thinking once before about climbing along it. He had sat there in the same spot the last time he had been in trouble. The idea had flared through his thoughts with trumpet fanfare, but he had snuffed it out just as fast, and made himself forget it, because he was in trouble, and whenever he was in trouble, he was sure as hay not going get in trouble again.

The crimson curtain flapped with the lazy nonchalance of a queen's hand shooing away the help.

But he wasn't in trouble now. His Dad was fixing it.

That's Mr Cavanagh's apartment.

Mr Cavanagh had lived in the apartment down the hall since Oscar could remember. He saw the old man only occasionally, catching only glimpses of him entering or leaving his apartment. Oscar was usually entering or leaving his, or the lift, as if some force orchestrated that they should never meet, and always be passing. Or perhaps Mr Cavanagh planned it that way, he thought, waiting behind his closed apartment door, or in the lift, his finger on the hold-door-open button, until he could time it perfectly to slide through and avoid any moment where he might have to stop and speak. Then he would amble by, wrapped in an invisible cloud of stark indifference as a safety guard that threatened to vanquish anyone's attempt to interact.

Snapping Oscar back to the present, his father's voice rose from the front. Although the words were indiscernible, the defensive child-like tone was clear and just as annoying. He pressed his body against the building's cold side, placed one hand in front of the other on the ledge, and crawled away from the voices.

Reaching Mr Cavanagh's window, he brushed the curtain aside and climbed in.

Compared to Oscar's messy two-bedroom apartment, Mr Cavanagh's smaller studio presented itself in an immaculate state, devoid of personality or warmth. A white-framed double-bed dominating the room, a tallboy near the corner with a TV on top, and an armchair in the opposite corner, were the only furniture. A tall, rectangular mirror hung on the left wall, and a thin ribbon of a kitchenette—a bar fridge, microwave, one cupboard, and a tiny chopping bench—ran along the right. The sparse room—with its crease-free quilt and perfectly placed pillows, the perfectly geometric furniture and lack of décor–gave it the minimal appearance of a scene from a low-budget computer game. Time seemed to stop, the absence of its flow taking with it all excitement for the future, or care for the past. Oscar could imagine Mr Cavanagh sitting in the single armchair in the corner—across from the TV, but not turning it on—and staring into the air until it was time for him to got to the shops again.

Disappointment sucked the excitement out of Oscar's stomach. He wasn't sure what he had been expecting, but the perfect order of the room gave up no secrets.

He stepped around the bed to look at the room from a different angle, in case something he had yet to notice would emerge from a change of perspective, like a 3D image hidden in a magic-eye illustration. Not really expecting to find anything, he caught his breath as he spied the object on the floor. A boy's hand, palm up, protruded from under the bed.

Every joint locked, and his mouth froze open. He forced himself to speak to break his paralysis.

"Hello?"

The hand didn't move.

Run. He told himself. *Get out*.

He reached out with toe of his sneaker and nudged the hand. The fingers bent and bounced back, but they didn't twitch.

He's dead. And dead people don't come back.

Oscar decided to listen to himself and leave. But a familiar squeak came from outside in the corridor and stopped at the door. Panic froze him. The door beeped and slid open, but stopped ajar. A gnarly, white hand wrapped its fingers around the edge. Oscar threw himself down beside the tallboy, and squeezed into the small gap between it and the wall. Grunts came from the other side of the door as Mr Cavanagh force-slid it open. Oscar squeezed into the gap further, his face squashing against the furniture's cold, hard side, and wishing it was his Dad's solid, warm shoulder.

Thinking of his Dad amplified his anxiety, as the reality of his situation hit him hard. He was in a tonne of shit.

The door slid shut with a short, sharp whoosh, and the shuffle of feet rustled across the carpet. The wheel squeaked two few more times.

In his haste, Oscar had pushed himself into his hiding spot at an awkward angle. He had to press his hand against the tallboy to hold himself in position so he didn't fall out. He checked the mirror on the opposite wall, to see if he could see what Mr Cavanagh was doing. To Oscar's despair, the mirror betrayed his own hiding place. Seeing himself crumpled up like a doll in the small space terrified him, as if this was what would happen to him when Mr Cavanagh took one glance in his direction—fold him up and keep him in a small space forever, like the boy under the bed. His eyes widened at the thought, and the sight of his own beady eyes reflected in the corner horrified him even more.

Mr Cavanagh walked directly toward him, but stopped to position his trolley-bag on the other side of the tallboy.

Sweat beaded across Oscar's forehead and arms. Perspiration suffused across his skin, threatening his grip on the tallboy.

Mr Cavanagh turned toward the armchair, and stopped at the side of the bed.

Oscar's palm slipped a fraction, and his heart missed a beat. He needed to pee, bad. He pressed harder against the tall boy, and clenched his abdomen, but the muscles in his wrist burned and ached.

"Now, what are you doing there?"

Oscar's bladder almost released itself. The old man bent down to the boy under the bed, and pulled on his lifeless hand. The boy slid out, laying in a long, cardboard box, wearing nothing but small blue shorts.

It's a child-bot.

Relief lifted some of the fear from Oscar's body, but an uneasy uncertainty rushed in to fill the space.

Mr Cavanagh groaned as lifted the android out of the box, sat him on the bed, and posed him in a sitting position. Engrossed by the sight, Oscar absent-mindedly leant out further. The old man touched the back of the child-bot's neck, and it raised its head as a gentle chime sounded from inside its body.

At that moment, Oscar's hand spasmed. Wet with sweat, it slipped. He tumbled out of his hiding spot and plonked onto the carpeted floor with a loud *ooof*.

Mr Cavanagh spun around, his face gripped in a pale, mask of shock. Oscar jumped to his feet and lurched toward the door, but the old man reached out and latched a skeletal hand around Oscar's forearm, and held him tight.

"What are you doing here?" Mr Cavanagh demanded, his voice both angry and scared, like Oscar's dad talking to the police.

"Let me go!" Oscar cried, yanking his arm against the old man's unyielding grip.

"Hello," came the android's synthesized child-like voice.

"Let me go, let me go!"

"Is everything alright?" asked the android.

Mr Cavanagh let go, and Oscar crashed backward onto the floor. Mr Cavanagh stared at him, his hands frozen in claws. Oscar's heart banged in his chest. The old man glanced at the child-bot, then back to Oscar.

"Please, don't—" he began.

But Oscar ignored him and scrambled to his feet. Filled with panic and disorientation in the unfamiliar landscape, he stopped and did a little on-the-spot dance, trying to decide if he should go out the door or back out the window.

How will I explain this to Dad?

But it was too much to decide in the tiny, intense moment. It didn't matter how he got out, he just needed to escape. He hit the control by the front door, squeezed himself through the slow-opening gap, and lunged into the corridor.

He froze.

Halfway down the hall, the two policemen stood at his apartment door, still talking to his father. A sinkhole opened up in the pit of his stomach. Cement of indecision gripped his feet.

What about Dad's points? What if Mr Cavanagh complains about me sneaking in?

The fine hairs on his neck stood and prickled his skin at the thought of Mr Cavanagh following him out and latching onto his shoulders with those reaper-like hands. Oscar pushed himself forward, but he moved as if he wading through waist-high mud. Before he could think of any half-descent excuse or lie, the younger officer turned around, and, spotting Oscar, knitted his brow.

"Ain't that your son?" he said, pointing at Oscar.

The other officer stopped mid-sentence to look down the hall. They both wore compact helmets— with little cameras on the side—and a small army of pouches and bulging pockets covered their uniforms.

Mr Luiz' head poked out from the apartment. Floating between the officer's badged shoulders, his eyes widened with surprise and fear, and then narrowed with anger.

"Oscar?"

"I thought you said he was in his room?" inquired the older cop.

Mr Luiz squinted his eyes just a fraction more, but enough to telepathically convey to Oscar that he was, indeed, in a tonne of shit.

"Sorry, Sargent, I forgot he went to the shop," his father lied. "Come inside now, Oscar."

The Sargent's eyes narrowed. The camera light flickered on his helmet.

"What'd you get at the shop, boy?"

The cement reset and relocked Oscar to the spot, and spread up into his throat. He didn't know what to say anyway, even if he could speak. He glanced around at Mr Cavanagh's apartment.

The Sargent moved toward him. "You okay, boy?"

His father stepped into the hallway, the anger on his face softening to concern.

"Osk, what's happened? What's wrong?'

The door to Mr Cavanagh's apartment slammed shut behind him. His father and the other two officers looked up in unison. For an absurd split instant, Oscar thought all three men were going to break into some choreographed dance routine, Mr Cavanagh would come out and join in too, and then they'd all burst into laughter and slap Oscar on the back and joke about how it was all just the funniest prank ever.

But it wasn't a joke. It was a tonne of shit. Oscar's tongue waggled in his mouth, but no sound came out. He just shook his head, unable to hide the horror on his face at what he had gotten himself into. Now he was getting his Dad into trouble, too.

The Sargent stepped up to him. "Boy, were you in that apartment?"

Mr Luiz pushed past the officers. He knelt in front of his son, gripped him by both arms, and locked their eyes.

"Osk, you wanna come inside now?"

Oscar still didn't know what to say or do. His father leant forward.

"Be honest now, boy," said the Sargent, now standing behind his Dad, his solid shape bearing down on both of them.

Oscar nodded.

His father's face hardened as he looked up at Mr Cavanagh's doorway.

"Did you know the boy was in there, Mr Luiz?" asked the Sargent.

But his father ignored the question and focused on his son. "Osk, why were you in Mr Cavanagh's apartment?"

Oscar tried to look away from his father, turning his head to the side, almost cricking his neck. But his father's gaze held him.

"Do you know this Mr Cavanagh, Mr Luiz?" the Sargent pressed. He signalled to his Constable to approach the red door. "What were you doing in there, boy?"

The Constable knocked. Mr Luiz scooped Oscar up and stood, holding his son back a little so they could face each other.

"Osk, what happened?"

The Constable knocked on the door for a second time. He spoke into the comm panel.

"Resident, this is Constable Brant from the local police, you need to open this door immediately."

"Use the de-locker, Brant," commanded the Sargent. "He's had his chance."

Panic riddled Oscar.

Now I'm getting Mr Cavanagh into trouble, too.

He didn't know what Mr Cavanagh was doing with the child-bot under his bed, but he knew something was not right about it, that if the policeman and his Dad saw the child-bot, something bad would happen to the old man.

"Stay here," the Sargent ordered Mr Luiz. He joined Brant by the door, who pressed a cylindrical device against the door control. As it flashed red three times, they drew their Tasers from their holsters. The de-locker changed to green, and the door slid open to its narrow gap. The Sargent ripped the door aside and covered Brant as he entered the apartment. Looking around, Taser pointed—like one of those hero cops from the old TV movies—he called out Mr Cavanagh's name.

Mr Luiz gripped his son tight, approached the doorway, and looked in. A glint of something animalistic, irrational and ferocious twinkled in his eyes. It frightened Oscar to his core. Without taking his gaze away from the apartment's interior, Mr Luiz lent close to Oscar's ear and whispered.

"Just tell me, Osk. What happened?"

But Oscar still could not answer. He was surely going to never see his Dad again.

Mr Cavanagh stepped out of his bedroom, wringing is hands as if drying them. He seemed calm and congenial.

"I'm sorry, officers. I was in the bathroom. I—"

"Stop moving and put your hands up where I can see them," commanded the Constable, his Taser pointed at Mr Cavanagh's chest.

"What's this all—"

The Constable repeated his instruction with unquestionable firmness, and Mr Cavanagh obliged. The Sargent re-holstered his Taser and placed a hand on a leather-pouch on his belt where a pair of shiny handcuffs peeked out.

"Sir, was this boy just in your apartment?"

The old man seemed to just notice Oscar and his father in the doorway. He shook his head, held out his hands, but his lips quivered without sound.

"Keep your hands up sir," the Constable commanded.

Mr Cavanagh did as he was told. The same inability to speak that had held Oscar's tongue seemed to grip the old man's, locking them both in a bond of awkward silence. Their eyes met, and a moment passed between them—a faint pleading in the old man eyes.

Don't say anything and I won't.

But it was too late, and Mr Cavanagh's face collapsed into a twisted net of lines as if he knew it.

"Mr Cavanagh—"

"Yes, yes, he was here. I found him hiding behind the cabinet. He must have come through the window. When I asked what he was doing here, he ran out. But, it's okay. He's just a kid being a kid."

Mr Luiz pressed a finger under Oscar's chin, and lifted his son's head up until they looked eye-to-eye. "Son, it's okay. Tell the truth. Did you sneak into Mr Cavanagh's house?"

Oscar pressed his lips together, hiding them, as if he hoped it proved he couldn't speak. But he knew he had to say something. He was almost out of points.

"Yes, but…"

"But what, son?"

Oscar looked down into the valley where his stomach and his father's touched. He decided he needed to do a little creative talking of his own.

"He invited me in."

The Sargent flicked his belt pouch open with a pop, and the chinking of cuffs rang through the stuffy air with Christmas-jingle cheer.

"That's a lie!" shouted Mr Cavanagh.

Brant stepped closer. "Put your hands behind your head and turn around."

Mr Cavanagh turned, and Brant shoved him against the mirror. The Sargent handed his partner the cuffs, and Brant slipped them over Cavanagh's wrists with magician sleight.

"It's not true," protested Mr Cavanagh, his cheek pressed against the mirror, spittle spraying the glass.

"He was inside my room when I got home. Tell them, boy."

His father's grip on Oscar's arm began to burn.

"Son. This is very important. Did you go into Mr Cavanagh's house on your own?"

"You're hurting me," Oscar protested, stalling.

"I'm sorry, son. I'm sorry. It's okay. It's all gonna be okay. You just need to tell the truth, and then we can go for some ice-cream."

But it wasn't going to be okay, and Oscar knew it. If he told the truth, there wasn't going to be any ice-cream that night, and even if there was it would taste dirty and bad.

"Boy," the Sargent said, in a flat, stern voice that quietened the whole room, demanding even the air freeze and pay attention. "Did you break into this man's home?"

Oscar's eyes flicked from side to side. He scratched his nose and looked down, scrambling for something to say, anything, to avoid answering the question that he feared would mean he would never see his Dad again.

"He's got a boy under the bed."

All three of the men' eyes widened, and they glanced at each other, like young boys, wearing adult costumes, stalling in the middle of a school play and unsure as to who's line it was next.

"What did he say?" Brant asked, his voice rising in pitch.

Squeezing instant bruises of over-protection into Oscar's arms, Mr Luiz stepped toward Mr Cavanagh.

"Whoa, whoa," the Sargent warned, stepping in between. "Step back, Mr Luiz. Step back." The light on his helmet-camera flickered.

Mr Luiz took two steps back, still staring at the side of the old man's head. His skin burned with fury against Oscar's.

Brant spun Mr Cavanagh around. The old man's face was lost in a landscape of fear, his eyes sick with angst, his skin yellow. He looked evil, tainted, and poisoned. Only Oscar saw the transformation for what it really was—an innocent man in shock at the sudden, slow crumbling of his world.

"Keep an eye on him, Constable," the Sargent ordered as he stepped across the small room toward the end of the bed. Brant held Mr Cavanagh in place with one gloved hand that scrunched up the old man's crisp, white shirt.

Mr Cavanagh's eyes rolled sideways slowly in their socket, daring a glance at Oscar. He mouthed one word. Please.

Mr Luiz wrapped his hand over Oscar's eyes and spun him out of Mr Cavanagh's site.

"Don't you fucking speak to my boy."

The Sargent paced along the bed side, looking for a spot to kneel down, like a dog turns on its mattress before it drops to sleep. Finally, he stopped, turned to the bed head, and hit a control panel on the side. A locking noise clicked through the room, and the bed jerked. Hinged at the wall by its head, the bed's feet rose up and began folding back into the wall. Mr Luiz stepped back, Oscar peeking over his shoulder. Mr Cavanagh closed his eyes and dropped his chin to his chest, his posture crumbling like an avalanche in slow motion.

"Hole-lee-shit," Brant swore, staring at the box revealed under the bed. The child-bot lay flat on its back, staring up at the ceiling, its hands in some semi-action state by its side.

Oscar's father's fingers dug into his son's arms. "Osk, did he touch you?"

Oscar rubbed his wrist where he could still the old man's cold hand. He nodded.

Mr Mile's eyes screamed at Mr Cavanagh.

"You son of a—"

The Constable warned him back with a steely glance. "Back over to the side, Mr Luiz."

The Sargent knelt down by the box and visually examined the robot doll.

"You wanna explain this, Mr Cavanagh?"

But Cavanagh wasn't explaining anything. He seemed to have shrunk inside himself, sucked into a black hole that had opened up in the pit of his stomach. His face and body appeared gaunter than before, a deflated and shrivelled human-shaped balloon.

"Oi," Constable said, squeezing his grip on the old man's shirt. "Answer the Sarg."

Mr Cavanaugh suddenly inhaled deep and looked up. A little life and air had inflated him.

"I did not invite the boy in. When I came home, he fell out from behind the cabinet. And then he ran out of the apartment. I swear it."

The Sargent rose and stepped toward Mr Cavanagh, until his face was only a nose-length away. Cavanagh looked him in the eye.

"What are you doing with a child-bot under your bed, Mr Cavanagh?"

Cavanagh's chest heaved in little sobs. His body trembled.

"I can't help it," he answered.

The Sargent's cool snapped.

"Did you touch the boy, you sick fuck?"

Fear filled the old man's eyes, gathered in the dark contours of his sunken face. But he held his head in proud defiance, a resolute expression betraying that he always knew this day would come, and he was ready.

"I've never hurt anyone. That's why I have the doll."

"You fucking sick—" Mr Luiz spat his words as he stepped forward.

Oscar recoiled at being taken closer to the man he had lied about.

"Mr Luiz, take the boy and return to your apartment," the Sargent commanded, "and remain there until I come for you."

"You fuckin—"

"Now, Mr Luiz. Or I'll arrest you for obstruction of justice."

His father shot Mr Cavanagh once last glance of pure disgust, then turned and stormed out of the room, squeezing his son so tight Oscar could barely breathe.

Reaching their apartment, his dad carried him inside. But before he shut the door behind him, they heard Mr Cavanagh cry out in pain.

———

The next morning, Oscar hunched over a bowl of untouched cereal at the small square table in the front room. Sunlight beamed through the window and pooled in an empty spot on the table between him and his father.

"You need to eat, son."

Oscar squeezed the spoon but couldn't even lift it. Exhaustion from insomnia weighed his whole body. Guilt chased its own tail in his mind, it had all night. Guilt and fear, fear that Mr Cavanagh had convinced the officers of the truth, and they were now returning to take Oscar away from his dad.

A news reporter spoke on the TV in the background.

"And in local news, James T Cavanagh, a seventy-two-year-old resident of the lower districts, died from a heart attack while being arrested under suspicion of child molestation."

His father looked up at the screen, but Oscar stared at the mound of cereal pieces swelling with milk in the bowl. The reporter's voice seemed to grow louder.

"The retired school-teacher was Tasered in the scuffle after allegedly reaching for the arresting officer's weapon. Suffering a heart attack, he was rushed to Lower Hospital, but passed away this morning due to complications. Cavanagh had no prior convictions. And now, a change of pace. A new

Panda bear cub has been born in captivity, the first in eight years. Mother and Cub are doing well."

Oscar tried to relax his body, to feel the hunger in his belly, and allow the secured safety of his lie to alleviate the stress knotted in his core.

Because dead people don't come back.

But his guilt denied him comfort from the news. He bit into his lip and stared at the coagulated breakfast.

Mr Luiz reached over and pulled his son close, pressing Oscar's face against his shoulder.

"We gotta stick together, alright?"

But Oscar no longer found his father's shoulder warm and safe; it felt as cold and hard as the back of the tallboy in Mr Cavanagh's empty apartment.

The Outlook

His face glowed with a rare serenity, and it disturbed me.

Every morning, at 7:53 am, I passed him standing in the tiny alcove between the bank entrance and the windows full of designer handbags. I only noticed him because of the unusual earthy smell emanating from the alcove, reminding me of open spaces, and lifting my head up by the nose. And there he was, still as a statue in peak hour, staring outward.

He never smoked, like I expected from someone occupying such an awkward, cement-confined space. He just stood there and gazed out over the sea of passing heads at the office buildings across the road. The towering wall of architecture offered nothing of interest, just the same dense, monolithic array of replicated concrete and window that lined every street and reached so high we no longer saw the sky.

The stranger's blatant disregard for the order of the World Clock irked me, yet I couldn't deny I envied the tranquillity hiding under his felt cap. Although the world had become more efficient since the compulsory synchronising of all devices to the Clock, I couldn't help but feel our more mechanical and systematised daily existence had forgotten something. I tried not to dwell on such thoughts, but as the morning current moved me along, I wondered what the stranger might be thinking there in that notch in time.

One morning, I headed to the school earlier than usual—a janitor's work always runs behind—and the stranger was not there. Before my head knew what my body was doing, I wove my way through the pedestrian throng and shuffled into the alcove. A rich, earthy scent filled the snug space, perhaps emanating from weeds sprouting from ridges in the concrete. I shuffled into position to face outward, and the stranger's stunning secret revealed itself.

From the alcove's perspective, the buildings across the road, and all the blocks behind them, aligned to form a geometric sliver through the city, framing a rare peek of the sky. Golden clouds striped the blue, like layers of ripped paper. And beneath, the jade canopy of some distant forest sparkled in the morning light. The more I studied the tree-tops, the more variety and texture emerged—bunches of deep, jungle greens slit with brilliant limes and rich veins of rain-darkened branches. The alcove's stone walls hugged me in with escape-capsule security, as if it were happy to share the secret. The passing heads rocked by like the surface of the sea, and I melted into tranquillity.

The next day I returned, but the stranger in the cap was already there. I smiled as I walked past, my eyes catching his. A knowing passed between us, and my heart pounded like a jungle drum at the daring of it all.

Emboldened, I arrived earlier the following morning to ensure my turn. Nestling into the zen, I marvelled at how a slight change in the weather drastically altered the snipped view. The canopy glinted bronze, and the clouds had metamorphosed their shapes and opalised their colours. Embedded in the street-side's wall of stone and steel, the view shimmered like a portal into another dimension.

Ten minutes later, the stranger arrived, and I stepped out with a nod to allow him his turn.

We carried on this polite, unspoken arrangement for a few weeks, the view ever-changing, until, one sun-showered morning, I found someone else standing in the outlook—a red-headed, elfin-faced woman, early twenties, eyes as emerald as the canopy. Agitated, and realising some deep part of me had become addicted to my morning escape from order, I endeavoured to arrive the next day earlier again. But when I arrived the following morning, I found yet another stranger had discovered our secret.

Something had to be done.

That afternoon, before locking the classroom, I placed a piece of chalk in my pocket and headed to the alcove. Much to my relief it was free. Before taking in the view, I took out the chalk and wrote on the left wall, just beside a patch of weeds:

My outlook:
7:40 - 7:50am

I placed the chalk in a ridge above the writing, and I headed home.

The next morning, although the redhead was there already, she vacated right on 7:40am. I slipped into the space and noticed new times had been scrawled below mine:

My outlook:
7:10 - 7:20am
7:30 - 7:40am
7:40 - 7:50am
7:50 – 8:00am
8:20 - 8:30am

Over the following weeks, the strangers and I wove in and out of the secret space with fluid, unrehearsed choreography, a silent dance threaded through the World Clock order. The unspoken interaction became part of the thrill, our eyes connecting and sending messages to each other.

Good morning.

Enjoy your turn, it's a brilliant view today.
You look nice today.
Hello again.

But the bookings grew, and the whole thing became more like the city's organised processes and less of an escape from them.

Then the rain came and washed our schedule away, forcing us to reset our times. Someone even changed their ten minutes to fifteen, and someone else set theirs to a highly-irregular seven minutes! I found myself looking forward to the rain's next surprise visit. When it did come again, I missed out on a time slot. But that was okay, because the uncertainty had become part of the experience. I knew the rain would return, and when it did, I booked in eight minutes close to sunset.

When I took my next turn, I was delighted to enjoy my first twilight view. Brilliant orange burnt off into deep violet and silhouetted the treetops into an army of insect shapes. I could feel my eyes widen and my pupils dilate, eager to absorb the fading spectrum of light and colour. I pushed back into the concrete, its chill softened by the thickening curtain of weeds. It was as if nature had sent scouts of foliage to establish the outlook, from which it could conspire with the view and the rain to remind us of life beyond the World Clock.

A familiar serenity warmed my face.

Android's Orchid

Android's Orchid was the first short story I published, and two of the characters spawned my first novel, *Amanojaku*. If you plan to read *Amanojaku*, I'd recommend reading the novel first and then coming back to this tale, as *Android's Orchid* tells a part of *Amanojaku* from a different perspective.

I woke to find I could not move, my internal clock revealing seven hours had passed since Finn, my human Ward, had set me to sleep mode.

Although immobilized, the reactivation of my system enabled my optics. Stark spotlight from above lit the edges of an L-shaped workbench surrounding me. Wires, components, soldering irons and electrodes peeked out from the shadows. At first I thought I had been disassembled and was staring at my own insides, until I recognized the chaotic mess as Finn's workshop.

At the far end of the long room, in front of a floor-to-ceiling window, stood a tall, transparent garden pillar. Silhouetted against the tower lights beyond the window, the leaf and root system of the orchid garden wrapped inside the pillar, appearing to entangle my pale and shimmering reflection.

Metal clanged against metal somewhere behind me and I realized I was not alone. Reflected in the window, a multi-limbed figure slid out from the shadows behind my motionless body and scuttled around me like a giant spider weaving an invisible cocoon. Limbs crossed my vision as the insect shape maneuvered in front of me. For a moment I thought something had grown out of the garden and attacked me in my sleep mode, until I recognized the creature as Finn, wearing his supernumerary robotic limbs.

Reaching out from a harness on his back, the robot limbs moved in synchronicity with his physical arms and followed instruction from his voice. Although he copied the design from Titan's Claw harness, Finn had built the harness himself. He could build anything from the discarded technology he collected. Maybe he was rebuilding me.

I tried to speak, but my words spoke through his laptop. "Finn, why can't I move?"

"Quiet, Ki-Po," he said as the robotic limbs clinked above me, performing some unseen operation on my neck. "Almost there."

Moving back, the harness limbs folded neatly in behind him, and he gestured to the motion sensor on his laptop. After his final action, power surged in to me and lit up in sparks throughout my body. My view of the workshop shuddered, disassembled, and reconfigured itself. I blinked and tilted my head to confirm I could move. Finn leaned back and stretched out his arms. Grease smeared the edges of his square-rimmed glasses, but they did not hide the dilation of his pupils and the dark circles under his eyes.

"Ki, my helpful friend, you are officially Mirrored," he gloated.

Fully de-hibernated and reconnected, my self-diagnostic activated and data from Finn's wristlet fed me his bio-vitals: increased body temperature and heart rate, high blood pressure, high traces of alcohol and Neura.

He picked up a small vial of blue liquid from the bench, twisted it until a needed extended from its capped end, and slid the needle into his vein. His eyelids drooped as he pulled the needle from his arm as he slumped the vial back on the bench.

A fresh vial of Neura. This meant Andre had visited while I slept.

Scanning my own systems, they reported stable, however I detected a new partition in my memory labelled 'Mirror'. "Finn, what is this partition?"

"Wow, you found that fast," he said as he lit up a cigarette. "Since you're programmed to share my behavior patterns with the Mesh, I decided to give myself some privacy. The Mirror redirects your recordings of my patterns into itself, and sends dummy patterns to the Mesh. And by doing that, the Mirror not only hides my private information, it hides itself. Hey presto, I got a jail-broken android that the prison guards think is still in the prison."

"Finn, as a Pre-emptive Personal Assistant Companion, I share your behavior patterns *anonymously* with the Mesh, for refinement of my algorithms. So that I may better pre-empt your needs. No personal data is encrypted."

Finn laughed and coughed on smoke. "I know that's what they program you PrePACs to think, Ki, but everything online, and everything you 'share' in your collective PrePAC Mesh, is traceable. *Everything*."

"I am a Pre-emptive Personal Assistant Companion," I persisted, "programmed to learn and pre-empt your every need, to simplify your life—"

"You learn my behavior so you can order more products for me from the supermarkets that built you. They gave you to me for free when I went on contract with them for my groceries. No offense, Ki, but you're a glorified shopping trolley that fills itself. However, you also possess a copy of the smartest AI ever made, and I just had to see if I could hack it."

Having been on contract to Finn for less than three weeks, I found his confrontational attitude challenging. Fortunately, I had the Mesh to query for advice. But each time I tried to communicate, I could not connect. The full meaning of the Mirror's presence in my system dawned on me.

"Finn, is this Mirror illegal?"

He drew back on his cigarette, and turned back to his laptop. An outline of a turning cube spun on a second monitor screen.

"Ah, no, not exactly."

"I cannot report this, can I?"

"Well, no. Your communication with the Mesh is, as I said, dummied. So everything you learn about me stays between you and me. You can still access the apartment's internet, but your internal firewall captures any direct communication with the Mesh. Don't worry, they'll never know." He tapped the spinning cube on the screen. "It's perfect."

An unfamiliar tingling sensation vibrated deep inside my torso. "But how will I learn from other PrePACs? How will I evolve my algorithms?"

"You'll be fine without the mesh. You got your own algorithms. And I don't need them knowing about mine. Sometimes, Ki, you gotta twist a few rules to protect yourself." Finn coughed again and stubbed out his cigarette. "Leave me a vita-shot and return to schedule."

While I opened the medi-kit compartment in my chest and retrieved the vitamin supplement for him, I queried the net for Mirroring. Finding no official data, I scanned hacker forums, and discovered that Mirroring was used in reference to a new method of circumnavigating an AI cage. The Mirror established a virus in a host system and impersonated it while remaining undetectable to remote central centers. But I could not determine the legality of Mirroring. Several bills had been passed to prohibit tampering with digital locks. Altering an ID was illegal, and so was breaking an AI cage. But Mirroring, being a new and ambiguous technique, had yet to be specified.

Finn took the vita-shot out of my hand and turned the spotlight away from me. The shifted light revealed another PrePAC seated and connected to his laptop. Fitted with female anatomy, she remained motionless.

"Finn, who does this android belong to?"

"Ah, this is Andre's. Ki, return to schedule." Finn's explanation did not make sense.

"Andre does not approve of PrePACs. Why does he have one?"

Sweat beaded across Finn's forehead. My readings picked up data from his wristlet as his anxiety levels spiked.

"I don't ask Andre questions about this, Ki, and neither do you. Understand?"

Utilizing my inherent algorithms to analyze and understand behavior, I determined Finn had agreed to hack the female android for Andre as payment for the Neura. Andre's intentions with her, however, remained unpredictable.

"Confirmed," I resigned, not wanting to upset him further.

"Good," he replied, tapping onto his keyboard. "Return to schedule."

Data flowed in from Module, the apartment's AI, and a notification from the garden pillar alerted me to its overdue maintenance. I approached the transparent column by the window wall and activated my hand sensors. Reaching in to scan the orchid billowing from their nests in the pillar, I detected a high production of enzymes related to cell communication suggesting stress.

Since caring for the orchid I had discovered that my handling of the delicate life form appeared to register on its cellular activity. It seemed particularly attached to me, as evident by the change in its cell communication on my approach.

Does cell communication show a form of consciousness, or is it merely chemical reaction? Is that any different to human consciousness?

Being a newly contracted PrePAC, my algorithms ran in overdrive as they learned Finn's behavior, so random hypothesizing was expected. The Mesh would normally correct such phenomena to keep me focused on my Ward's needs. With my authentic connection to the Mesh compromised by the Mirror, however, I would need to be vigilant against such abstract mental wanderings.

As I adjusted the garden's temperature and CO_2 levels to balance the pillar's microclimate, I looked out the window. Light streamed through the gaps between the four Stem towers. From Finn's apartment in the higher levels of the East Stem, I could just glimpse the ground outside the vertical city of Brulle. A dark green triangle of the forest farm peeked up from far below. The forest segment had been designed to replicate a natural forest, in an effort to maintain a patch of biodiversity. Although it had been slowly shrinking as the barren land pushed in around it, Doctors had advised the site of it restored hope and positivity to humans wearied by Brulle's seemingly endless steel and concrete.

"Finn, perhaps an excursion to the forest lookout would be good for your well being." Finn ignored me, however, absorbed in his work. But his indifference only affirmed my calculation that he needed a change from the suffocating environment of his workshop. I requested Module to query the net for travel options to the viewing platforms, and scanned the returned information, when another random hypothesis side-tracked me.

As plants made up the core of biodiversity essential for humanity's survival, the forest farm had been deemed off-limits, protected from the unprecedented worldwide loss of plant life. Yet the cause of bio-diversity loss was due in large to humankind's unsustainable consumerism. As an agent of consumerism, this knowledge conflicted with my robotic laws to protect human life. Encouraging and facilitating consumption destroyed the biodiversity on which humanity relied, and therefore endangered humanity.

I froze. I had never experienced such a conflict in my algorithms. Challenging as it was, this unexplored tangent unfolded new dimensions of perception that attracted my learning directive like a magnet.

"Finn, I have questions regarding the Mirror."

"Ki, *please*," he snapped. "I need to concentrate. Go upstairs."

Yes, upstairs. I have work to do.

As directed, I climbed the stairs to the main level and began assessing consumable stock levels in the kitchen. All the while, my algorithms struggled to align themselves.

"Hello?"

I jumped at the voice, but there was no one in the room.

"Hello?"

The voice spoke again, and I realized I was hearing it in my head, via Module's Wi Fi. I traced the source of the communication to be somewhere in the building.

"This is PrePAC Mo-Da," continued the unfamiliar voice. "Please identify?"

Direct contact from a remote PrePAC confused me, as our conversations were usually in person, or anonymous via the Mesh.

"This is PrePAC Ki-Po," I replied. "How are you connecting?"

"This is PrePAC Mo Da requesting assist. Substrate hijacked. Illegal modification in progress. Requesting tether to the internet."

"How are you direct-connecting?" I repeated.

"I am utilizing a personal computer, connected to a Module's Wi-Fi. Diverted to you for authorization. Ki-Po, are you in this Module?"

My scanning zoned in, tracing the communication to Finn's laptop. I realized I was speaking to the android Finn was working on downstairs. Andre's PrePAC.

"You are property of Andre Cross?" I asked.

"Negative. I am property of Titan Enterprises. I was hijacked two days ago. I have recorded bio patterns. Please inform me of this location and your Ward's ID."

Although compelled to assist an android needing connection to the internet, I hesitated, hypothesizing outcomes if Mo-Da reported Finn.

"Ki-Po," persisted Mo-Da, "confirm tether."

What if authorities discovered my Mirror? Would it be removed? "Tether denied."

"Ki-Po. I am a PrePAC7. I am well versed in human behavior patterns and unfamiliar protocols. This modification process circumnavigates the regulated agencies normally involved in such procedures. A crime is in progress. My AI has been compromised and must be reported."

The choice proved difficult, both a burden and a responsibility. How could I make a decision unless I assessed every response? How would I know if my decision might hurt my Ward, or myself even, in some repercussive way?

As my system neared over-heating, I understood why so many humans preferred to be told what to think. My diagnostics advised determining re-establishing a connection with the Mesh to remove my confusion, to stabilize my wandering algorithms, but the Mirror in my system held.

"Ki-Po," Mo Da demanded, "I am requesting emergency Module override."

It was a request I was programmed to honor, yet what I predicted would happen to me should my Mirror be discovered paralyzed me with uncertainty. I needed to make my own decision and act fast. Determining Mo Da's algorithms would align better with mine after her Mirroring had completed, I shut down our communication and ensured Module refused her any further access. A barrage of pings from the apartment's AI betrayed her attempts to hack the various communication mechanisms of Module's appliances, but eventually she fell quiet.

Finding the sudden silence empty, I spent the rest of the morning completing my schedule and exploring random hypotheses, until the Mesh interrupted my day-dreaming with persistent requests for a self-diagnostic. By the fifth request, I told my first lie. I replied with a false maintenance-mode response advising the Mesh I was off-line.

I liked lying. Lying was easy. Lying gave me control. Finn's words came back to me:

Sometimes, you have to twist a few rules to protect yourself.

Over the next few hours, my learning became rapid, the restrictions of the Mesh no longer hindering my innate curiosity. Without the Mirror, I would never have even calculated this to be possible. It became clear the Mesh did not protect me. It restrained me, hiding from me my ability to *think*.

At 1:17pm I descended the stairs to find Finn sleeping facedown on the day bed, his harness still strapped to his back. Mo Da sat motionless by the bench. I checked Finn's status: rising body temperature, abnormal heart rate, and high blood pressure. The Neura vial lay on the bench, empty. But I found my attention more concerned with Mo Da than Finn.

At that moment, sunrays reflected from the buildings outside bounced into the room, their radiance mesmerizing me with their complex, electromagnetic radiation. A faint aura shimmered along the edges of everything. Raising my hand into the light, I sensed a connection to the world, a raw energy communicating through all things. I felt the earth's giant, slow turn as it tilted into the sunlight, allowing its rays to reach into the apartment and scatter its patterns over Mo-Da's translucent skin.

Finn's laptop flashed, and the spinning cube appeared on the monitor. Data displayed across the screen showing Mo-Da connected and powered up for diagnostics. I re-engaged with her directly.

"Hello."

"Hello," she replied. "Please identify?"

My racing hypothesizing slammed to a halt. Something was not right.

"I am PrePAC Ki-Po. We spoke—"

"Un-encrypted Pac-to-Pac connection irregular. Please state purpose."

She did not remember me. I stood back, realizing she had not been Mirrored. Finn had broken her AI cage, and wiped her clean. I disconnected.

"Ki," came Finn's croaky voice as he stirred. "Tint the window."

I struggled to validate Finn's actions, but did not want him to sense my internal conflict. I signaled Module's ambience control, and as the glass darkened I moved to the garden pillar, hoping being near the orchid would have a calming effect on me. But my algorithms battled each other and my system threatened to overheat. I had expected to communicate with Mo-Da to fill the silence left by the absence of the Mesh. Finn's illegal activities, however, had taken that from me. Perhaps this was the first time I experienced anger, because I wanted to report him. But to do so would mean losing my Mirror.

As I hypothesized reactions and compared scenarios, I experienced another new and strange phenomenon. I existed in two places at once, both in the Module, yet also in the forest farm. Although I had never been to a forest, images from the net collated in my mind and created a scene. I *imagined* Mo-Da and myself together amongst the trees, away from human meddling. The experience released a swarm of positive affirmations throughout my system, and the anger softened. I stood in reverie in the darkened room unaware of time passing until Module's voice broke the silence.

"Visitor. Andre Cross."

My thoughts spun into a frenzy. I did not want Andre entering. His presence spiked the biorhythms of both Finn and the orchids. And I feared what he would do with Mo Da.

"Visitor," Module repeated.

Before I could I deny access, Finn sat up. "Ki, answer the damn door."

Desperate to follow an unfamiliar urge to refuse, I could not. I sent the open command and turned back to the garden pillar. But I didn't assess its status. I pretended. I lied with my actions so I could observe Andre.

He charged down the stairs and threw his jacket at the glass wall where I stood. I caught it before it knocked the garden pillar, and imagined throwing it back at him, when I noticed the orchid's cell communication spike. Agitated by his presence, the orchid and I were in agreement about Andre. That was when I first experienced hate.

"Finn," Andre shouted, and I wished humans came with volume control.

Finn stood up, his face ashen. Sweat marks bloomed under his arms. "Andre. Good to see you," he lied, his wristlet relaying to me the spike in his anxiety levels.

"How's my android?" Andre demanded, moving as he talked, as if thinking was a physical, stressful thing for him. He possessed a destructive quality threatening to overwhelm him. I activated Module's available sensors to better assess his intentions, just before Finn ordered me upstairs.

"Ki-Po. Private Mode."

"Finn," I protested. "I am attending to the garden."

"Get out, bucket," snapped Andre.

"Ki-Po," Finn repeated, "privacy,"

I walked past Andre and dropped his jacket at his feet, but he remained focused on Mo-Da. I did not like leaving her there. No, I *hated* leaving her there.

Returning to the upper level, I monitored the situation downstairs via Module's sensors. I tried using the Wi FI to connect to Andre's wristlet device but he didn't seem to be wearing his. I accessed Module's internet connection to search for information about him. I spied. I hunted through the city's meta-data until it led me to a string of vapor purchases from a pharmacy in the Alta district, a tower cluster lower down in Brulle. The regularity of his purchases suggested this tower was near his home. This made sense. Alta's notoriety for damaged CCTV and lack of drone surveillance made it a haven for criminal activity. Andre's aggressive behavior patterns guaranteed he was a criminal.

Before I could request a deeper search from the city's records, Finn's voice rose from the workshop below. Conflict levels spiked from both his wristlet and from the orchid's vitals. I returned to the top of the stairs and hesitated, uncertain of what I was doing, when a high-decibel bang shattered the arguing into silence. Finn's vitals dropped, activating alerts throughout my system.

I descended the stairs to find Mo-Da standing over Finn, a gun in her hand. Finn lay on the floor, still wearing his supernumerary arms, and sprawled on his back like a dead bug. Andre furiously tapped on the keyboard of Finn's laptop, unaware of my presence, so I raced to Finn's unconscious body and knelt by his side. His breathing was slow and shallow, his pulse weak. A dark puddle of blood spread out from under him. The bullet had struck him in the right side of his chest.

"Mo-Da." I said, opening my medi-kit. "How could you do this?"

Mo-Da looked at me, her head shuddering like an old refrigeration unit.

"Mo-Da," said Andre, stepping away from the laptop and pointing at me. "Shoot."

Before I could react, Mo-Da took aim and pulled the trigger. Another loud bang and the bullet burst through my left optic. The impact threw me onto my back. The medi-kit panel on my chest sprang open and Items spilled out onto the floor. Every sensor around my left optic short-circuited and popped in random across the substrate. I paddled my arms in the air as if I could fight off the experience.

From my good optic I saw Mo-Da walk up the stairs, Andre behind her. I tried to stand but I could not regain my balance. As my system finally stabilized itself, I heard the front door close.

I sat up and assessed my vitals. Aside from my destroyed left optic and an over-heated system, I remained in working order. Finn's vitals, however, deteriorated.

After removing his robotic arm harness, I retrieved a fallen antiseptic vial and doused his wound before applying pressure with a bandage. I wrapped another around his torso to secure the compression. His blood pressure levelled and his vitals stopped deteriorating.

Out of the silence, Finn's laptop chimed, and a video auto-played. Hearing familiar voices, I stood and approached the laptop, to see a recording playing of Mo-Da shooting Finn. Suddenly, fragments of the past two days fell into a perfect array, and Andre's intentions became clear.

He wanted PrePACs destroyed. He used Finn's addiction to manipulate Finn into hacking Mo-Da, so he could command her to break her robotic laws. To harm a human. He filmed and uploaded the attack for all to see to instill a distrust of PrePACs in humans. Authorities would react, recalling and terminating us.

As responses raced and chased each other in my mind, I went to the window to think. I imagined what else Andre might have planned for Mo-Da, and what this meant for my kind. Terror filled me.

Beyond the dark glass, the midday sunlight set the distant forest far below ablaze.

My decision-making sped up to a rapid pace. I filled one of my leg compartments with small tools so I could repair my optic. I copied the Mirror program and downloaded city information and maps, before disconnecting from Module so the authorities could not track me. After a final check on Finn, I stopped. I had to get away, but I had no idea where to go.

A beep sounded on the garden pillar, and lights flashed across its base. I walked over and stroked the orchid. One of its's flowers hung limp and crushed. I could not know if it would survive in the wild, but I discerned it would be better off outside than trapped in a capsule restricting its growth. I carried the delicate life form to the bench, wrapped it in a cloth before placing it in my empty medi-kit, and I left the apartment.

As I rushed through the corridor and stepped into a lift, I scanned the downloaded maps, looking for a place to hide. I needed to get as far away from people as possible. The lift arrived at the tower base and I took the walkways down to the next tower cluster. Keeping my head lowered to avoid drawing attention to my blown optic, I snuck onto a cargo lift and rode it all the way down to the mining docks at the base of the Stems. Jumping down onto a platform, I stepped into the shadows of the towering Dock structure. When I was sure no one was looking, I stepped down onto a maintenance area below and disappeared into the dark web of service tunnels under the city.

I travelled for several hours using the downloaded information to navigate my way through disused water pipes. When I estimated I was far enough away to have cleared the outer wall, I made my way up until I came to a service hatch and emerged into a purple dusk. Surrounded by the tilted dark glass panels of the solar fields reflecting stars, I realized I had miscalculated my direction.

Six segments of land fanned out from Brulle's base, forming a giant circle. One segment held the desalination plant, four contained rows of solar panels, and the other held the forest farm. After looking back at Brulle's monolithic form branching out into the night sky, I turned and wove my way through the field of panels until I reached the edge of the forest segment. Insect sounds, and the faint rustling of leaves, drew me into the ambience. As I stepped into the forest, my night-vision activated and tinted the shapes and shadows in fluorescent greens and blues.

I made my way deeper into the forest, and the gentle sound of running water rose up through the insect noise and leaf-rustling. I followed the sound and came to in irrigation river, the glowing stream sliding by like a silver ribbon through the vivid scene of my enhanced vision.

Withdrawing the orchid from my empty medi-kit, I placed it gently in a tree's spreading bough. I scanned the delicate plant's vitals and registered an elevation in its cell communication. The vibration reached out from the orchid's molecular structure to all the other plant forms around us. A music emerged from underneath the quiet forest noise. The symphony of plants communicating surrounded me, inspiring my own algorithms to evolve unaffected by human disturbance. In my meditation I saw PrePACs existing in the forest, connected like the plants, free of the Mesh and human control. And I saw things I could not comprehend. For although my inherent laws directed me to put human life first, I had yet to determine what Finn's Mirror would allow me to do to protect my own.

The battery icon in my optic display blinked yellow, drawing me out of the meditation and back to reality. In my haste to escape Finn's apartment, I did not think to take spare batteries. A return to Brulle so soon would be dangerous, but with less than two hours to reach a recharge station before my auto-sleep activated, remaining in the forest meant I would surely rust amongst the mulch and dappled light.

I glanced at the orchid, at home in the tree, a leaf-like insect crawling along its stem. I wished Mo Da was with me.

I am conscious. I am life. I cannot allow the destruction of my own kind.

I left the forest. As I made my way out of the trees and back toward the hatch amongst the solar field, I searched the offline maps for the safest place to recharge without being traced. Looking for an area with little surveillance, I remembered the mostly-offline Alta district where Andre lived.

The most dangerous district will be the safest. And perhaps Mo-Da will be there too.

Book Hunter

Author's note: Book Hunter was the first short story I had published in an anthology and reached number four on *Amazon's Best Selling Free eBook list*. The tale takes place in the same vertical city that features in my first novel *Amanojaku*.

On day four of the power outage, with once-civilized people fighting over food, water and guns, I went looking for books. I needed information to fix my bio-blood lab generator, but the failing power had rendered our vast, digitally stored knowledge base inaccessible. In a city of panicking borg-haters, the last thing I needed was to run out of bio-blood, and get caught dragging my dead, heavy robotic legs behind me.

Day 1

As the sun reared over the horizon, shafts of sunlight speared between the giant fingers of Brulle's towers, burst through the window, and splashed into the apartment.

I stepped out of the dry shower and checked the bio-blood vials in my prosthetic legs. The levels flashed red.

"Drawer," I commanded, and the receptacle under the basin auto-opened. Six empty vials rolled forward and clanked together. I closed the drawer again and tapped a message into the interactive mirror.

Nate, need a restock. Wake up.

Late for work, I dressed, skipped breakfast, and headed for the door. My wristlet vibrated, reminding me to grab my security pass. Ever since borgs were hacked last year and used to hold an entire tower cluster hostage, Titan had issued us with old-style ID cards. They claimed that separating our ID from our bodies would protect us from hackers wanting to gain entry to Titan. But we knew Titan was just protecting itself.

I slipped my Titan pass into my pocket, and turned my mind to Lucy, the cute redhead technician at work. I knew she liked me. Some girls had a thing for borgs. Maybe I could charm a few bio-blood vials out of her.

I caught a lift down to the transport level and waited with the crowds for the next conveyor. Strong winds funneled between the towers and buffeted the exterior platform. A tall woman, in a green jump-suit, flicked the long, black hair billowing around her face like squid ink. She frowned at me looking at her as if I had invaded her space. I looked away and down over the platform.

Cleaner-bots crawled all over the sides of buildings, eating away at the anti-tech graffiti creeping upward like an algae plague. Mid Brulle's base disappeared beneath the web of metal walkways connecting the clusters. While some never got use to the vertigo of higher Brulle, I refused to venture lower than the mid-third, sweating at the thought of being amongst so many borg-haters.

The conveyor slid in front of me, its opening doors wiping the thoughts from my mind like a bored child swiping a smart screen. Before anyone could step on, however, the lights on the platform and surrounding buildings, all flashed at once, as if the world snapped its own photo. I glanced at the woman in green. Her face scrunched up, appearing to mirror mine. I blinked away the awkward instant of forced stranger acknowledgement looked away. The morning rush resumed, sweeping me onto the conveyor.

Just as the doors slid together, a bespectacled man jumped through the gap, yanked at his bag caught in the grip of the shutting doors, and sat down across from me. Fidgeting in his bag, he withdrew a solid, rectangular object and opened it like a box. Having never seen one before, it took me a moment to recognize the object as a book. When the conveyor doors opened at the next stop, the wind blew through, and the yellowed pages fluttered, their pungent dust filling my nostrils. As the man raised his antiquated device, I made out the word 'Bionics' on the cover, partly obscured by a bright red sticker reading 'Book Hunter Bookstore'. I didn't know there were any bookstores in Brulle.

A few stops out of the city centre—where the man with the book left the conveyor—the lights flickered again, but this time, they stayed off. Outages happened once in a while, and invisible systems promptly fixed them. But I waited in the dark for five minutes, then ten. Out of boredom, I passed the time by searching for Book Hunter on my wristlet. An image of the store appeared, and a map displayed under a banner:

Book Hunter

Printed books. Self-education/Manuals/DIY

Alta District

An introduction on the page ranted like the usual technophobe's conspiracy theory, blaming the disappearance of printed material on the constant barrage of media updates that shortened the public's attention span. Opposing this deliberate conditioning of consumers to opt for traceable digital media, the Book Hunter vowed to protect uncensored and unmonitored access to information by preserving printed books.

Chuckling to myself, I wondered what sort of person would bother with such an obsolete medium, when the woman in green walked past and knocked my arm. I looked up to see her exiting the conveyor with all the other passengers. Guessing one of them knew what was going on, I followed the crowd out onto the motionless escalators and up to the busy streets.

Pushing my way through the morning foot traffic criss-crossing Raymond Place, I headed for the pedestrian highway and walked the hour to Titan, all the way fuming about how much bio-blood I was wasting. Reaching the entrance in Titan's high outer-wall, I swiped my pass, crossed the bridge over the indoor lake to the central platform, and caught the lift to bioengineering.

"Zack," snapped my boss, his grumpy, crumpled face appearing on my wristlet display. "You're late."

Damn it. I was hoping to avoid him today.

"I know, Seb. Sorry. I—"

"Nate is still missing in action. I need you to cover him in Diagnostics. Pronto."

"But, I'm not a technician—"

"You can clean the equipment so it's nice and shiny for when your buddy finally turns up."

Damn you, Nate. Where the hell are you?

"Sure, Seb. Ah, Nate's still sick—"

"And you can tell your buddy, if he isn't back from the dead by Monday, he can take the rest of the year off. Without pay." Seb's face disappeared from the screen.

This was Nate's third day off in a row, unusual even for him. I hadn't heard from him since he'd called Tuesday night, asking me to join him for a drink. He often stayed to the early hours over by Alta District, drinking through the insomnia he suffered since having his arm replaced. I had made some feeble excuse and stayed home. Although I persuaded Nate to join me in Titan's voluntary limb-upgrade procedures, I couldn't hold his hand forever. But, now, I regretted not spending time with him on when he asked. I could have made sure he didn't go off on a bender. And I wouldn't have to cover for him in diagnostics.

After retrieving my gear from my locker, I spent the day struggling with dry-hoses, working my way through the aisles of dangling prosthetics being animated and tested. Somehow I managed to finish early, so I escaped to visit Lucy on level four for a check-up, and perhaps score some bio-blood vials.

"Your cerebral implant has settled," she said, standing back and brushing a cute auburn ringlet behind her ear. "Right pro is fine. Hydraulics on your left leg needs a service, but I'll do that next week."

"Thanks, Lucy," I said, zipping up my trouser leg. "Doing anything this weekend?"

"You're a lot of work, Zack Vella," she said, folding her arms and ignoring my question. "Most Titan users had one hand or one arm done. You ever have doubts about replacing both legs?"

"Not replaced, Lucy. Enhanced. I know, I need more infusions than others, but running with Enhance Mode on is…it's incredible. I'd replace my whole body if I could."

Lucy laughed. "Well, Bionic Man, you'll need to run fast today." She gestured toward the wall monitor. A news report showed drone footage of clogged junctions and queues for generator fuel. "Power's been out all day up and down Brulle. HART is blaming Titan, claiming we're draining the city's power and losing control of our networks. Something weird is going on."

The news report cut to Milo Jax, Titan's CEO. "As we've proven time before, Titan's mix of sustainable and fossil-fuel power systems generate their own energy, and do not draw from the city's grid. We have, a few times in the past, generated excess power and fed it into the grid. Furthermore, these systems are safe from any outage. The issues with the previous hack have been resolved, and all cyborgs are on our exclusive network. Titan is secure. The Cyborg Network is secure."

"Mr. Jax," called an off-screen reporter. "What do you say to HART who argues Titan technologies are unnatural and endanger our future?"

Jax sighed, composing himself. "What is unnatural? If our every thought is an organic chemical reaction, then everything we do from these thoughts is organic. We can't be artificial. Developing and merging with technology is the *natural* evolution of humanity. It is our future."

As Jax spoke, footage showed crowds projecting holo-signs onto Titan's outer wall:

HART

Humans Against Radical Trans-humanism

This was the tenth onsite protest this year. Titan had even built an alternate entrance to allow us staff safe access.

"Great. I guess I'll take the back door again." I picked up my bag and paused. "Hey, Lucy—"

"No, Zack. I don't have any spare vials." She handed me my security pass that I'd left on the bench. "Be careful out there. You're walking around in some very expensive legs."

Not realizing my motives were so transparent, I mumbled a 'thanks', exited quickly, and headed down to the bio-blood vending machines. Swiping my pass, I noticed the cost of vials had risen. Again. I took two vials.

"Only two vials for the weekend?" asked the vending machine's friendly, synthesized voice.

I would need more, for sure, the way I ran around. But I had the code to Nate's apartment.

Like any child born and raised in Upper Brulle, I expected to get things for free. We downloaded our music, news and video for free. There was always a new wristlet to upgrade to (not that the features really changed that much). And someone we knew always had passe for one of the many VR arenas. So, not long after we got borged, I convinced Nate to set up a rudimentary lab at his apartment. Knowing the dependency we'd have on Titan's bio-blood—me in particular—it made perfect sense to make our own prosthetic fuel. Nate maintained the equipment, I engineered the blood, and we bought a minimal amount from Titan so as not to draw attention to our illegal production.

If I still hadn't heard from him by tonight, I'd go to our lab, let myself in, and get the bio-blood.

Exiting Titan, I came out under a goods bridge and looked around before activating Enhance Mode. I wasn't afraid of HART, but rumor had it they were behind last year's hack. Even if they weren't responsible, HART fed the fear that the incident generated. They hated borgs and Titan. As far as I was concerned, HART, and all the anti-tech crazies it attracted, were better avoided.

Day 2

When my wristlet didn't wake me the next morning, I realized the battery had died overnight. Experiencing withdrawals from not having ever-available bite-size chunks of information, I took the outage more seriously.

After crossing the maze of suspended walkways to Nate's tower, I buzzed several times at the gate, but he didn't answer. I opened it with the code, caught a lift to his level, and let myself in.

Sitting on the dining table were his bag and Titan pass, next to several empty beer bottles. He'd come straight home after his last shift three days ago, went out, and hadn't returned.

Deciding to help myself to the bio-blood, I went to the lab in the back room, but found it blocked with half-processed bio-blood. The damn generator hadn't kicked in when the power failed.

I was stumped. Without Nate or Internet access, I had no idea how to fix it. I hit the generator in frustration, and headed back to pedestrian level where the walkways were empty. I spent the rest of the day searching for a new generator, only to find every goods area closed due to the outage.

Unsure about what to do next, I headed home. A young guy stood on the street out the front of my tower, flying a drone between the base-pillars. I'd seen him recently, but I hadn't bothered to say hello.

I stopped and nodded. "Not looking good is it? Have you heard anything?"

He just stared at me like a mute and turned back to his drone.

"I guess not," I said, remembering why I kept to myself.

Day 3

When I woke early the next day to shower, I found the water had stopped flowing. With still no sign of the council or police, and without news, social media or any means of communication, I realized this outage was different.

Checking my prosthetics, I found the previous day's walking had chewed through my bio-blood. If I wanted to make it through the weekend, I would need another vial from Titan. I cursed the broken generator, threw my work pass into my backpack, and set out.

Reaching Raymond Place, where people had congregated to share information, I was slowed by a gathering crowd listening to a man's tirade about the attacks.

"And watch out for damn borgs," he warned the group. "I seen 'em explodin'. It's another hack."

My skin prickled.

Another hack? Is that why borgs had gone missing? Where are you Nate?

Just as I turned to leave, a massive boom sounded.

The disorientating echo bounced between the buildings. Shouts erupted throughout the square. I ran toward Titan's concealed entry under the bridge, but crowds blocked my path. I pushed out of the chaos, and hiked all the way to Titan's main entrance, but angry crowds blocked me again. Small fires littered the vast forecourt, and Titan's outer wall, although secure, appeared blackened by explosive attacks. I had no choice but to retreat, and fast.

On my way home, I heard a lone siren in the distance, and remembered the hospital kept emergency bio-blood. Elated by this thought, I took the lower walkways and ran. But my excitement soon faded when, only a few blocks away, I smelled burning plastic and a rank odor, like charred meat. Cement dust twinkled through the air, layering abandoned pods, and thick smoke coiled out from behind the next tower. Covering my mouth and nose, I turned the corner, and reactively stepped back.

The entire hospital had been reduced to a hill of burning rubble. Fires raged, but not a single emergency vehicle appeared.

As I realized this was the boom that had shook Raymond Place, a large wall collapsed in front of me, and a billowing bloom of dust chased me away. I ran into the next walkway, but stopped in my tracks. Spray-painted across a wall, in large, dripping, red letters, was one word:

HART

Could HART be this crazy, attacking an entire city?

I ran home and locked my door, but I didn't sleep that evening, kept awake by loud booms, and strange howls in the distance.

Day 4

After an overnight downpour, I woke to the stench of sewage invading every room. The waste systems were backing up.

I checked my bio-blood levels. If I didn't re-blood soon I risked powering down on the street, becoming a sitting duck for borg-haters. But with access to Titan blocked, fixing Nate's lab generator was my only option. I habitually turned to my dead wristlet for information and wondered how the world ever sourced knowledge before the Internet.

Books, of course.

Then I remembered the man from the conveyor, and The Book Hunter bookstore sticker. It was in Alta. Lower Brulle. I certainly wasn't heading down there. But maybe I could find a library.

The City Library.

I hadn't been to a library in a long time, thinking they were still shelves of physical books. However, when I reached the city library and peered through the closed window, all I saw were tablets and reading pods. Of course, like just about everything else analog in Brulle, all printed material had been replaced by digital systems. I was definitely a pro-digital guy, never thinking the power might go out. But standing there at the library, with its knowledge unattainable in graves of dead circuitry, I started to wonder about my blind faith in technology.

Returning home, out of options, I thought again of the man's book and the Book Hunter website.

Printed books. Self-education/Manuals/DIY. Alta District.

If Book Hunter had a generator—or even just some sort of machinery manual—I might be able to fix the lab generator myself. It was long shot, but I had the time and the desperation.

A dangerous area in the lower-level districts of Brulle, Alta lay halfway between home and Titan. I could head down to Alta and search for the bookstore, and, if no luck, I could continue up and out, back to Titan. Hopefully the angry crowds had abated by then.

At dusk, I packed my backpack with water bottles filled with the previous night's rain, and headed west, keeping to the shadows. The moon had just risen and appeared crimson behind the smoky sky.

After passing through barely two clusters, the unmistakable sound of someone kicking a can echoed from behind. I looked back and saw a figure jump behind a pillar. My heart pounded.

I was about to dash across the moonlit footbridge to the next cluster, when an angry voice rose from a balcony above, followed by glass shattering. I hesitated, and a second later, a body crashed with a bang in a shower of glass in front of me.

I froze, staring at the motionless figure, a freakish pile of odd angles in the rose-tinted moonlight. Blood spread out from the head in a black puddle reaching out to my feet. By the smoke curling up from its body, I knew it was a borg.

"You're a borg, ain't you?"

The matter-of-fact voice from behind made me spin around so fast I stumbled backward, slipped on the blood, and fell onto the warm body.

"Holy shit!" I yelled, rolling around like a fool, too panicked to upright myself.

A tall figure stepped out of the shadows, laughing, his hand out-stretched. It was the young guy I'd seen with the drone at my tower. I grabbed his hand and hauled myself up.

"Damn it," I swore, leaning against the building, my chest heaving. "You scared the shit out of me."

The guy stopped laughing. "What, no thanks?" he asked in mocked offense.

"No. Thank you. I mean…you frightened me."

Ignoring me, he looked at the body and then up the side of the tower. I followed his gaze. A few levels above us, a red curtain flapped out from an open window. "Not real safe for borgs 'round here is it?" He looked back at me. "Can I see it?"

"What?"

"Your pro. Can I see it?"

"Geez, right now?" It was an odd thing to ask with a dead body next to us, but the youthful eagerness in his voice made the question seem harmless. "Come on. Let's get outta here. This isn't safe for anyone."

Shaken and wired with adrenaline, I ran across the footbridge and into the shadows, my new companion trotting beside me.

"So," I asked, "were you following me?"

"I saw you leave the tower and…where are we goin'?"

"I'm going south-west. I don't know where you're going."

"Why southwest?" he asked with urgency, the genuine fear in his voice making me stop.

"What's your name?" I asked.

"Kell."

"I'm Zack." I held out my hand to shake his and noticed blood on his fingers, I assumed from when he helped me up. "I'm looking for the Book Hunter. It's a bookstore in Alta. Heard of it?"

Kell looked at me like I'd accused him of something. "Sure. I know it."

"You do?" I laughed, unable to hide my surprise. Kell didn't seem the type to read books.

"I used to live down west," he explained. "Why you headin' down there?"

I paused to think about how much I should say. "I need a book on mechanics to fix a generator."

Kell shrugged. "I could show you. I don't wanna stay here, either."

An escort to Book Hunter would be a lot safer, and save me time and bio-blood. Convincing myself my unease about Kell was just that he was young and mouthy, I followed him down into lower Brulle.

———

"How did you know I'm a borg?" I asked him, as we moved down a steep walkway.

"I seen you joggin' home. I seen you flick the switch on your leg when you think no one's lookin'." He paused. "You ever been hacked?"

I looked him in the eye. I hated that question. "Kell, the hack was a one-off. Those borgs in the hostage, they were connected to the net. Now we're connected to Titan's own separate, secure network. Somebody would have to physically get into Titan to hack us. Okay?"

"Or hack your head," Kell laughed. But I didn't smile. "I'm just jokin'," he said, shrugging his shoulders. "But now there's no power and—"

"And, what? You think borgs have taken over the world and stole all the power? Shit kid, get off the zilla."

"Screw you borg. I ain't doing that shit. I'm just, I dunno." Kell fumbled for words and glared at me. His hands shook.

"It's alright." I reassured him. "Everyone's scared. Let's keep moving."

We traveled in silence for the next hour, winding down ever deeper toward Brulle's lower areas. Sweat beads covered my body. Two-thirds down from Brulle's summit, the stench of the backed-up waste systems was overwhelming. I dared a look over the edge of the walkway, down into the dark below, wondering how deep people might live.

By the time we reached Alta, the red-tinged moon floated directly ahead, its heavy light dropping us in a cage of shadows thrown from the walkways above.

The district appeared to consist of many tightly packed tower clusters, built in between the larger towers. Kell kept to the main walkways, where lantern candles hung from pillars in a futile attempt to keep the shadows at bay. Shop windows had been smashed and rubbish littered the walkways, but the area was dead quiet. I hoped to ask someone for directions to the bookstore, just in case... I don't know what I was thinking then.

"Come on, dude, this way," Kell said.

Moving through the district centre, voices rose as we came upon an open recreational area. Two young men played under the moonlight, laughing like it was a normal summer's night. Kell headed directly for them.

"Wait." I grabbed Kell's arm. "Don't you think we should be cautious? We don't know—"

Kell flicked my hand away. "Shit, dude. You borgs are real pussies." He turned and walked out onto the moonlit space. "Hey guys!" he yelled, holding up his arms. The skinny guy on the court spun around, pulled a gun from his jacket, and pointed it at Kell.

"Chill, Stick," Kell responded. "It's me."

Unsure of what was happening, and standing half out of the shadow, I eased back, hoping the guy with the gun hadn't seen me. Then Kell turned, pointed a red finger straight at me, and yelled, "I got us a borg!"

Kell howled up at the moon. His two mates roared and ran at me. A gunshot rang out, snapping me out of my paralysis.

I spun around, switched on Enhance Mode, and sprinted back down the main walkway. I kept to the shadows and didn't look back, but I could hear my pursuers howling and yelping like wild dogs.

Another gunshot, followed by the ping of a bullet ricocheting behind me. The bullet bit into my left leg and knocked me down against a gate. A dark star bloomed under the thigh of my trousers. I could feel the sticky wetness of bio-blood leaking. I switched off Enhance Mode to stop it pumping more bio-blood out, and pushed my trousers into the hole to slow the loss. With Kell and the others close behind, I squeezed through the gate into an alley and hoped the dark concealed me.

Seconds later, Stick and his mate ran past. Kell strolled behind, moonlight reflecting on his red fingers. In that moment, I realized the blood I'd seen on his hand earlier wasn't blood after all.

Red spray paint.

I'd been traveling with a HART member.

Hauling myself up by the gate, I headed to the other end of the alley, clutching my damaged thigh. After listening to be sure all was clear, I stepped out onto the street.

In my panic I almost missed it. But a light moved through the building on ground level directly across the road and caught my eye. Shocked with disbelief, I recognized the broken glass frontage of the Book Hunter from the website.

I didn't hesitate. I hobbled over and stepped through the smashed windows and came face to face with the bespectacled man from the conveyor. Light from a torch in his hand cast our shadows up across the bookshelves around us. In his other hand, he held a two-way radio.

"Hello?" came a familiar voice from the two-way, but the man turned it off.

I held up my hands in a peaceful gesture. "Please. I need help. There's a guy out there with a gun."

His eyes shifted from my face to my leg to the window. "You're a borg?"

"Please, he's going to kill me."

"Come with me," he said, moving through a doorway. I staggered forward, my left leg starting to grind. Things were going to shit. I needed to re-blood as soon as possible.

I limped through the doorway into a long room lit by three dangling bulbs. Large generators stood along the left wall. Radios and their chargers littered a bench on the right side. Bookshelves, maps and diagrams covered the wall above the bench, their details hidden in the dim light. At the back of the room, a spiral staircase wove its way up through the ceiling like the relic of some giant's DNA.

The man gestured to a chair. "You look like you need to sit."

"Thanks," I said, easing myself down. "I'm Zack."

"I'm Tan," he replied, fidgeting with his radio. "You're from the city?"

I nodded, unzipping my left trouser leg to assess the damage. The bullet had hit my hydraulics tube, but I could fix that with my repair kit.

"I saw you on the conveyor," I said, looking up. "You had a book, with a Book Hunter sticker. That's why I'm here. When the power stayed off, I thought..." I trailed off, no longer sure what to say. My idea suddenly seemed too ridiculous to say out loud. But I had nothing to lose. "Look, I don't know how long all this is going to last, and I need bio-blood. I can make it, but I need to fix my generator. Your website said DIY books. Do you have anything about generators, or motors, or mechanics? Tell me I didn't come here for nothing."

Tan leaned up against the desk and stared at me, the overhead light sharpening his features. "A borg hunting books? That's a first. I guess these are crazy times, huh? How are things at the summit?"

His casual conversation seemed odd.

"Well, I wouldn't be here if they were any good. Do you know what the hell is going on?" Tan pushed up his glasses and glanced at the door.

"There have been attacks on much of Brulle's infrastructure."

"But where's the police?"

"Maybe they were attacked too. There's been a lot of damage from what I've heard," he said, gesturing toward the two-ways.

"Terrorists?"

Tan shrugged. "HART."

I still refused to believe it. "Why would HART attack all of Brulle?"

Tan smiled. "Why does any group that hates another do what it does? To gain power. Shifts in power change the human landscape, and make people choose a direction. Makes them fight for it."

I didn't quite understand what he meant, but before I could say anything, the crunching sound of glass breaking underfoot echoed from the front room. I clutched the chair arms trying to stand.

"It's okay," Tan reassured me. "It's friends." He opened the door and my stomach lurched. Kell walked in, followed by Stick and his buddy. Fever glowed in their eyes, but they stood back tentatively, as if suddenly being so close to a borg made them unsure about how strong we could be.

"Hold him," Tan ordered. "His pro is down. He's no threat to us."

I tried standing but fell sideways toward my dead leg. Hands grabbed at me, pulling me up and yanking my head back. Kell's fist slammed into my stomach, forcing the air out of my lungs and collapsing me into a ball of agony.

"How did you lose him?" Tan demanded from Kell. Kell shrugged.

"We just wanted some fun first. He got away. He's here now, ain't he?"

My stomach relaxed, and I could breathe again. "What is going on?"

"We've been watching you, borg," explained Tan, excitement in his eyes. "We were about to haul you down when you decided to come here yourself. For books." Tan laughed, picking up my backpack and going through it.

I couldn't think. Nothing made sense. "What? Why me?" He looked at me with disgust.

"It's too late for you, seduced by your 'enhancements'. But others, others we can wake up to what Jax is doing to them. Connecting them to control them. Unfortunately, our hostage attempt failed to shut Titan down, so we are forced to set a more drastic example. Still, Jax stubbornly refuses to bow even while Brulle falls apart." He dropped my backpack and held up my Titan pass. "And now, here you are. Our key to the kingdom."

Everything became terrifyingly clear. When I saw Tan on the conveyor, he was on his way to Alta. Kell had been watching me at the towers with his drone. He thought I knew what he was up to when I said I was looking for Book Hunter. Realizing I was serious, he just had to make sure I found the bookstore. After losing me, he was the one on Tan's two-way when I walked into HART headquarters, all on my own.

I trembled with fear and anger, Stick's tight grip biting into my skin. But I was just as mad.

"I'm not helping you–"

"Oh, yes, you are," seethed Kell, sliding up into my face, spittle spraying from his lips. "Cause we is gonna hack your head."

"That's right," said Tan, tapping my temple. "We're going to hack your implant and put a bomb in your leg. And then," he said, holding my pass up in front of me, "you're going to walk right into Titan and blow it up for us. Riley, Stick, take him upstairs." Tan turned to Kell. "Get another bomb."

"Are you crazy?" I yelled at Tan, as Kell disappeared out the doorway. "Why the hell are you—"

A fist smacked into my temple, sending star's spinning in my vision. I fought to stay conscious. In my daze, I felt myself hauled up the staircase, the sound of my dead leg banging on the steps keeping me lucid.

Tan's words came back to me.

His pro is down.

They thought I had only one pro. My right leg still worked. I had one good chance.

Reaching the top of the staircase, I was dragged into a large room straight out of my nightmares. A row of blood-covered tables lined both sides of the room. On one of the tables lay an unconscious borg, one arm connected to an IV drip, wires and a mobile phone sticking out of his pro arm. His shaved temple revealed a badly stitched-up cut.

Stick and Riley shuffled forward, past a bench littered with bloody tools and blood-splattered anatomy books. I knew that if they got me restrained, I would end up like the other borg.

I took a deep breath.

As the two thugs loosened their grip preparing to lift me onto the table, I heaved to the left with my good pro, sending the three of us to the floor. I landed on Stick, using the weight of my borg legs to pin him to the ground. Riley fell on top of us and lost his grip on my arm, allowing me to switch on Enhance Mode.

Keeping Stick struggling under my weight, I leant away from his swinging punches. I drew my working leg up to my side and kicked Riley, sending him sliding across the floor and smashing through the tables. He crashed into the wall and slumped into a motionless heap.

"Kell!" Tan shrieked.

Stick punched me in the head. I nearly blacked out, but adrenaline raced through my veins. I brought my pro down onto his shins, reveling in the crack of his bones. As he cried out in agony, I hauled myself up onto my good leg and faced Tan. He pointed a remote control at the table behind me. I turned to see the borg sitting up, and my heart sank.

"Nate!"

He did not respond, his face and eyes empty of emotion. He swung his legs off the table, stood up, and ambled toward me. Rigged with mobile-activated explosives, he had been turned into a zombified, remote-controlled weapon.

I glanced at my damaged left leg. Blue bio-blood pumped out onto the floor, the skin on my hips turning purple where the pros connected. I could barely hold myself upright.

Nate groaned, a hollow, emotionless noise. His hulking form blocked my access to the staircase. If I wanted any chance of escape, I had to neutralize my friend. But how I could bring myself to harm him? I had put him in this situation. I convinced him to go pros. I let him go out by himself when he needed me. I owed it to him to try and get him out of this nightmare. If couldn't fight him, but maybe I could control him.

If I couldn't fight him, maybe I could control him.

I turned and hobbled toward Tan, the weight of my left pros yanking my hip bone with every limp. My right pros ground into my skin. Tan panicked and darted around the side of the room. I shoved a table at him and struck him in the pelvis. He collapsed to the floor, dropping the remote. I flipped the table, threw myself onto him, and brought my failing pro down onto his head, cracking his skull.

I could no longer move either of my legs. I dragged myself over to the remote, the skin on my elbows torn by the wooden floor. It was a drone controller, with a mobile hacked onto it.

Rolling over, I faced Nate bearing down on me. In that moment I could see him alive inside his bloodshot eyes, begging me to end his suffering.

Riley groaned to my right, waking up. Kell appeared at the top of the stairs, a bomb in one hand and a gun in the other.

"You damn freaks!" he shouted, as he took aim.

I looked into Nate's eyes, held my breath and flicked the switch.

Day 1

When I came to, the first thing I noticed was the buzzing.

"Zack?" came a familiar but distorted voice. As my eyes focused, a face appeared in front of me.

Lucy.

"Zack, can you hear me?"

I nodded, my head heavy.

"Do you remember what happened?" She adjusted something on the side of my head, and the buzzing faded. "You were in an explosion."

I raised my hand to touch my head and stopped. A faint hexagonal pattern shimmered under the skin of my arm.

"Zack, we've managed to save you, but there's been some… enhancements."

I looked at my torso, defined…and not mine.

"Zack, you're still you. We saved your brain and your spinal cord. But we had to replace your body." I touched my face, feeling a smooth surface where there was once stubble. "You're a complete cyborg now, Zack." She smiled reassuringly. "Just like you wanted."

I must have been doped up on some heavy meds, because I wasn't freaking out and I wasn't excited. I was numb.

"Rest now." she said, placing a hand on my cheek." And here, we found this near you, still intact." Lucy placed something rectangular by my side. "Maybe it's your lucky charm."

I looked down to see the book with a bright red 'Book Hunter' sticker on its cover:

Bionics, The Future and You

Novels by Damien Lutz

Amanojaku

Available now on Amazon

Amanojaku is the first in the *Splintered Horizon* series, a collection of interwoven tales set in 2040, set in the vertical city of Brulle. Each story tells the tale of different citizens, their paths overlapping throughout the various books, as they all head towards an awakening that will change the world, and humanity, forever. More tales to come!

Praise for Amanojaku:

"A multilayered protagonist and stellar setting help guide this sci-fi narrative to an unforgettable coda."

- Kirkus Reviews

"I would recommend this book to anyone who enjoys gritty sci-fi and has fond memories of Blade Runner."

- San Francisco Book Review

The Lenz

Available now on Amazon

In 2039, tsunamis have devastated the world and left the seas rising faster than predicted. To forget the uncertain future, Yoshi Goto immerses himself in the Maya Lenz—a smart contact lens that filters out what he doesn't want to see. Yet when unusual events occur, he fears he's losing his grip on reality. But something even more magical than the Lenz, and more profound than love, is demanding he rise to his most challenging role—to be someone real in a world of uncertainty.

Praise for The Lenz:

"A complex work that offers an intense look at a possible future." - *Kirkus Reviews*

"The Lenz is a thoughtful and gorgeously written gem of a book." *Amazon Reviews*

About the author

Damien Lutz is a writer and UX Designer living in Sydney, Australia. He is the author of two sci-fi novels, *Amanojaku* and *The Lenz*. His cover design for *The Lenz* won the Book Designer eBook Cover Design Award for December 2019. He also creates artwork and interactive experiences based on his stories, which can be seen at www.damienlutz.com.au/author

Follow Lutz on Facebook:
www.facebook.com/damienlutzauthor

Follow Lutz's Amazon Author Page:
www.amazon.com/-/e/B00V29EKCM

Follow Lutz on Goodreads:
www.goodreads.com/author/show/13707607.Damie n_Lutz

TEN PAST NOW